Praise for the Parker series and Richard Stark:

"A winner . . . terrific . . . a taut slice-of-life mystery in-fused with a refreshing dose of randomness and the untidiness of real life. Stark's series is utterly enjoyable."
Kansas City Star

"This latest installment of the miraculously revitalized career of the master criminal Parker [is] great, dirty fun."
Publishers Weekly

"Donald Westlake's Parker novels are among the small number of books I read over and over. Forget all that crap about *War and Peace* and Proust—these are the books you'll want on that desert island."
Lawrence Block

"You can read the entire series and not once have to invest in a bookmark."
Luc Sante

"Parker returns, tougher than ever. . . . As Donald E. Westlake or Richard Stark, this crime novelist gives the best lines to the bad guys."
TIME

"The neo-hero: the ruthless, unrepentant, single-mind-ed operator in a humorless and amoral world. . . . No one depicts this scene with greater clarity than Richard Stark."

PARKER

Parker novels by Richard Stark

The Hunter (Payback)
The Man with the Getaway Face
The Outfit
The Mourner
The Score
The Jugger
The Seventh
The Handle
The Rare Coin Score
The Green Eagle Score
The Black Ice Score
The Sour Lemon Score
Deadly Edge
Slayground
Plunder Squad
Butcher's Moon
Comeback
Backflash
Flashfire (Also published as Parker)
Firebreak
Breakout
Nobody Runs Forever
Ask the Parrot
Dirty Money

Grofield novels by Richard Stark

The Damsel
The Dame
The Blackbird
The Sour Lemon Score

Information about the complete list of Richard Stark books published by the University of Chicago Press—and electronic editions of them—can be found on our website: http://www.press.uchicago.edu/.

PARKER

(Originally published as *Flashfire*)

RICHARD STARK

The University of Chicago Press

The University of Chicago Press, Chicago 60637
University of Chicago Press edition 2013
Printed in the United States of America

22 21 20 19 18 17 16 15 14 13   1 2 3 4 5

ISBN-13: 978-0-226-00225-5 (paper)
ISBN-13: 978-0-226-00239-2 (e-book)

Library of Congress Cataloging-in-Publication Data

Stark, Richard, 1933–2008, author.
  [Flashfire]
  Parker : now a major motion picture (originally published as Flashfire)
  / Richard Stark.
      pages cm
  Originally published as: Flashfire. New York : Mysterious Press, 2000.
  ISBN 978-0-226-00225-5 (paperback : alkaline paper) — ISBN 978-0-
  226-00239-2 (e-book)
1. Parker (Fictitious character)—Fiction. 2. Palm Beach (Fla.)—Fiction.
3. Jewel thieves—Fiction. 4. Criminals—Fiction. I. Title.
  PS3573.E9F57 2012
  813'.54—dc23
  2012010013
♾ This paper meets the requirements of ANSI/NISO Z39.48-1992
(Permanence of Paper).

ONE

1

When the dashboard clock read *2:40,* Parker drove out of the drugstore parking lot and across the sunlit road to the convenience store/gas station. He stopped beside the pumps, the only car here, hit the button to pop the trunk lid, and got out of the car. A bright day in July, temperature in the low seventies, a moderate-sized town not two hundred miles from Omaha, a few shoppers driving past in both directions. A dozen blocks away, Melander and Carlson and Ross would be just entering the bank.

The car, a forgettable dark gray Honda Accord, took nine point seven two gallons of gasoline. The thin white surgical gloves he wore as he pumped the gas looked like pale skin.

When the tank was full, he screwed the gas cap back on and opened the trunk. Inside were some old rags and an empty glass one-point-seven-five-liter jug of Jim Beam bourbon. He filled the bottle with gasoline, then stuffed one of the rags into the top, lit the rag with a Zippo lighter, and heaved the bottle overhand through the plate-glass window of the convenience store. Then he got into the Honda and drove away, observing the speed limit.

2:47. Parker made the right turn onto Tulip Street. Back at the bank, Ross would be controlling the customers and employees, while Melander and Carlson loaded the black plastic trash bags with cash. Farther downtown, the local fire company would be responding to the explosion and fire with two pumpers, big red beasts pushing out of their red brick firehouse like aggravated dinosaurs.

The white Bronco was against the curb where Parker had left it, in front of a house with a For Sale sign on the lawn and all the shades drawn. Parker pulled into the driveway there, left the Honda, and walked to the Bronco. At this point, Melander and Ross would have the bags of money by the door, the civilians all facedown on the floor behind the counter, while Carlson went for their car, their very special car, just around the corner.

When there's an important fire, the fire department responds with pumpers or hook and ladders, but also responds with the captain in his own vehicle, usually a station wagon or sports utility truck, painted the same cherry red as the fire engines, mounted with red flashing light and howling siren. Last night, Parker and the others had taken such a station wagon from a town a hundred miles from here, and now Carlson would be getting behind the wheel of it, waiting for the fire engines to race by.

Parker slid into the Bronco, peeled off the surgical gloves, and stuffed them into his pants pocket. Then he started the engine and drove two blocks closer to where he'd started, parking now in front of a weedy vacant lot. Near the bank, the fire engines would be screaming by, and Carlson would bring the station wagon out fast in their wake, stopping in front of the bank as Melander and Ross came running out with the full plastic bags.

Parker switched the scanner in the Bronco to the local police frequency and listened to all the official manpower in town ordered to the convenience store on the double. They'd all be coming now, fire engines, ambulances, police vehicles; and the fire captain's station wagon, its own siren screaming and red dome light spinning in hysterics.

2:53 by this new dashboard clock. It should be now. Parker looked in the rearview mirror, and the station wagon, as red as a firecracker in all this sunlight, came modestly around the corner back there, its lights and siren off.

Parker wasn't the driver; Carlson was. Leaving the Bronco engine on, he stepped out of it and went around to open the luggage door at the back, as the captain's car stopped beside him. A happy Melander in the back seat handed out four plastic bags bulging with paper, and Parker tossed them in the back. Then Carlson drove ahead to park in front of the

Bronco while Parker shut the luggage door and got into the back seat, on the street side.

Ahead, the three were getting out of the captain's car, stripping off the black cowboy hats and long tan dusters and white surgical gloves they'd worn on the job, to make them all look alike for the eyewitnesses later. They tossed all that into the back seat of the station wagon, then came trotting this way. They were all grinning, like big kids. When the job goes right, everybody's up, everybody's young, everybody's a little giddy. When the job goes wrong, everybody's old and nobody's happy.

Carlson got behind the wheel, Melander beside him, Ross in back with Parker. Ross was a squirrelly short guy with skin like dry leather; when he grinned, like now, his face looked like a khaki road map. "We havin' fun yet?" he asked, and Carlson put the Bronco in gear.

Parker said, as they drove deeper into town, "I guess everything went okay in there."

"You'd have thought," Carlson told him, "they'd rehearsed it."

Melander, a brawny guy with a large head piled with wavy black hair, twisted around in his seat to grin back at Parker and say, "Move away from the alarm; they move away from the alarm. Put your hands on your head; they put their hands on their heads."

Carlson, with a quick glance at Parker in the rearview mirror, said, "Facedown on the floor; guess what?"

4

Ross finished, "We didn't even have to say, 'Simon says.'"

Carlson took the right onto Hyacinth. It looked like just another residential cross street, but where all the others stopped at or before the city line, this one went on to become a county route through farmland that eventually linked up with a state road that soon after that met an interstate. By the time the law back in town finished sorting out the fire from the robbery, trying to guess which way the bandits had gone, the Bronco would be doing seventy, headed east.

Like most drivers, Carlson was skinny. He was also a little edgy-looking, with jug ears. Grinning again at Parker in the mirror, he said, "That was some campfire you lit."

"It attracted attention," Parker agreed.

Ross, his big smile aimed at the backs of the heads in front of him, said, "Boyd? Hal? Are we happy?"

Melander twisted around again. "Sure," he said, and Carlson said, "Tell him."

Parker said, "Tell him? Tell me?" What was wrong here? His piece was inside his shirt, but this was a bad position to operate from. "Tell me what?" he said, thinking, Carlson would have to be taken out first. The driver.

But Ross wasn't acting like he was a threat; none of them were. His smile still big, Ross said, "We had to know if we were gonna get along with you. And we had to know if you were gonna get along with us. But now we all think it's okay, if you think it's okay. So what I'm gonna do is tell you about the job."

Parker looked at him. "We just did the job," he said.

"Not that," Ross said, dismissing the bank job with a wave of the hand. "That wasn't the job. You know what that was? That was the *financing* for the job."

"The *job,*" Melander added, "the real job, is not nickel-dime. Not like this."

"The real job," Ross said, "is worthy of our talents."

Parker looked from one to another. He didn't know these people. Was this something, or was it smoke and mirrors? Was this what Hurley had almost but not quite mentioned? "I think," he said, "you ought to tell me about the job."

2

It had started with a phone call, through a cutout. Parker returned the call from a pay phone and recognized Tom Hurley's voice when he said, "You busy?"

"Not in particular," Parker said. "How's the wing?" Because the last time they'd been together, in a town called Tyler, Hurley had wound up shot in the arm and had been taken out of the action by a friend of his named Dalesia.

Hurley laughed, not as though he was amused but as though he was angry. "Fucked me a little," he said. "I feel it in cold weather."

"Stay where it's warm."

"That's what I'm doing. In fact, that's why I'm calling."

Parker waited. After a little dead air, Hurley did his

laugh again and said, "You never were much for small talk."

Parker waited. After a shorter pause, Hurley cleared his throat and said, "It's a thing with some people I don't think you know."

"I know you."

"Well, that's just it, I won't be there. If you want it, you're taking my place."

"Why?"

"I got a better something come up, offshore. I'm fixing to be a beachcomber. A rich beachcomber."

"Because of the arm," Parker suggested.

"That, too," Hurley agreed. "These three are good boys. They know how to count at the end of the day, you know what I mean."

Parker knew what he meant; they wouldn't try to hog it all, at the end of the day. He said, "Why don't I know them? They civilians?"

"No, they just work different places, different people, you know how it is. But then, it could pan out with them, and then you know them, and who knows."

"Who knows what?"

"What happens next," Hurley said.

Letting that go, Parker said, "Where are they now?"

"They move around, like people do," Hurley told him. "Lately, they're based around the Northwest somewhere, or maybe Vancouver. Over there someplace."

"Is that where this thing is?"

"No, they like to work away from home."

So did Parker. He said, "Not around me."

"No, in the Midwest, one of those flat states out there. I told them about you. If you're interested I'll give you a number."

So one thing led to another, and here he was in the back of the Bronco with Melander and Carlson and Ross, and after all he was going to be told the who-knows that Hurley hadn't wanted to talk about.

3

It's jewelry," Ross said.

Parker wasn't impressed. "That's a dime on the dollar, if you're lucky."

"That's right," Ross said, "that's what we'll get."

Melander said, "We got three buyers, ready to go. That's what they all give us."

Parker said, "Three?"

"There's too much for one fence," Ross explained.

Parker was beginning to get interested. "What are we talking about here?"

Carlson steered them up onto the interstate ramp as Ross said, "Four of us will walk home—"

"Ride home," Melander corrected him. "In a limo."

"Right," Ross agreed. "Four of us will ride home with three hundred grand apiece."

Parker looked from Ross to Melander and back.

They both seemed serious, if happy. Nobody in the car was taking any mood changers. He said, "This is twelve million in jewelry?"

"That's the floor," Ross said. "That's the appraisal. It's a charity sale. If we let it alone, it'll go higher, but what we'll get is the floor."

"A charity sale. Where?"

"Palm Beach," Ross said.

Parker shook his head. "Deal me out."

Ross said, "You don't want to listen to the job?"

"I just heard the job," Parker told him. "Twelve million in jewelry all in one place draws a lot of attention. Cops, private cops, guards, sentries, probably dogs, definitely helicopters, metal-detecting machines, all of that. Then you put it in Palm Beach, which has more police per square inch than anywhere else on earth. They're *all* rich in Palm Beach, and they all want to stay that way. And besides that, it's an island, with three narrow bridges, they can seal that place like it's shrink-wrap."

"All of this is true," Ross said. "But we got a way in, and we got a way at, and we got a way out."

"Then I still know the job," Parker told him, "and I still don't want it."

Melander said, "Just out of curiosity, why?"

"Because to even think about doing your job," Parker told him, "and to do it in Palm Beach, there's two things you got to have. One is the insider, who's the amateur, who's gonna bring you down. And the other is a boat, which is the only way off the island,

11

and which is even worse than an island, because there's no way off a boat."

Ross said, "That's yes and no. We got the insider, that's true, but he's *before* the job. He's nowhere near Palm Beach on the day, and he's not exactly an amateur."

Melander said, "He's one of our buyers, we worked with him before."

"What he is," Ross said, "he's an art appraiser, estate appraiser, he tells you what the paintings are worth, what the rugs are worth, what the jewelry is worth, for the taxes and the heirs."

Keeping his eyes on the road, Carlson said, "He has a little trouble with nose powder, so he needs extra money. But he doesn't let it make him a problem, at least not for us."

"What his occupation is," Melander said, "he spends his life casing the joint."

"Then he tips off you guys," Parker said.

"Right."

"And then you go in and take out the best stuff. And how long before somebody notices, when this guy does the appraisal, step two is a robbery?"

"We don't do it that way," Ross told him. "Our agreement is, we never touch a thing until at least two years after he's been and gone. And this time, the Palm Beach, he wasn't one of the appraisers."

"He gets access to the appraisals," Melander added, "like anybody else in the business."

"He's done other stuff in Palm Beach," Ross said, "so he knows the place, he knows the routine, he knows everything about it, but he isn't one of the people that looked at this particular bunch of jewels."

Melander said, "He's moved in that territory, but on different estates, different evaluations."

"If they're looking for an insider," Ross said, "they won't look at him, because he wasn't inside."

"Possibly," Parker said. "What about the boat?"

"No boat," Melander assured him. "I a hundred percent agree with you about boats."

"Then how do you get off the island?"

"We don't," Ross said.

"You stay there? Where? You know, you rent a condominium, the cops are gonna look at recent rentals."

"Not a condominium," Ross said.

"Then where?"

"At my place," Melander said, and grinned like a bear.

Parker tried to see around corners, but couldn't, not quite. "You've got a place there?"

"It's fifteen rooms," Melander told him, "on the beach. I think you'll like it."

"You've got a fifteen-room mansion on the beach in Palm Beach," Parker said. "How does this happen?"

"Well, I looked at it a few weeks ago," Melander said.

"But he's just buying it today," Ross said. "We got the down payment from that bank back there."

4

The motel, and the car Parker would be using, was in Evansville. When they got there, while Melander and Ross counted the money on the bed, Carlson and Parker sat in the room's two chairs, across the round table from one another, and Carlson told him more. "The mansion is cheap. I mean, for a mansion in Palm Beach."

"Why?"

"It was sold maybe eight years ago to this movie star couple, you know, he's a star and she's a star, so when they make a picture, he gets twenty million, she gets ten million—"

From the bed, Melander said, "Still not equal pay, you see that?"

Carlson and Parker both ignored him, Carlson saying, "They bought the place, they thought they'd be stars in Palm Beach, but Palm Beach ignored them.

14

They're stars, but they're trash, and in Palm Beach you can't be trash. Or, if you are trash, you hide it, and you spread your money around."

"Charities," Melander said.

"They love charities in Palm Beach," Carlson agreed. "But these stars didn't do it right. They thought they were already entitled. They threw big flashy parties, they brought in *rock bands,* for Christ's sake, and nobody came."

"Well, a lot of people went to those parties," Ross said.

Carlson said, "Not the right people. Also, the parties were playing hell with the house, messing it up. Then the stars went away to be stars someplace else—"

"Where stars are looked up to," Melander said.

"So the house was abandoned," Carlson said, "and the alarm systems would break down all the time, and bums would sneak in there from the beach, and they had a couple little fires, and the cops finally said, we can't keep a man on this house twenty-four hours a day, you got to put in your own security patrol, and the stars said fuck it, and put it on the market."

Laughing, Melander said, "A fixer-upper for sale in Palm Beach. A do-it-yourselfer."

"These stars couldn't do anything right," Carlson said. "If *they* do the fix-up, they make a lot more money when they sell the place. But they're not interested, they're off somewheres else, and the house sits there until Boyd comes along."

Melander got off the bed and took a stance, shoulders squared, big body relaxed, big smile, big wavy hair framing his head. He said, in a strong Texas accent, "I do like this little town you got here, I'd like to contribute if I could, make it even better. I like that ocean you got, you know, it's bigger than the Gulf, I like the idea of that whole ocean out there and then Europe on the other side, not Mexico. Not that I have anything against Mexicans, hardworking little fellas, most of them."

Melander sat down to the money again while a grinning Carlson said to Parker, "Boyd can fit right in. And with all that oil money in his family, he'll fix up that mansion good as new. Better. And when he's got the house all done, he wants to host the big library benefit there."

Parker nodded. "All right, he can be plausible," he said.

Carlson looked pleased. "So you're in?"

"No," Parker said.

All three were disappointed, gazing at him as though he'd let them down in some unexpected way. Carlson said, "Could I ask why?"

"You've got a place to stay," Parker said. "If I ask, you'll tell me how the mansion won't trace back to any of you after it's all over."

"Sure," Carlson said.

"But that isn't the job," Parker told him. "That's nothing but the safe house. The job is still a whole lot of jewelry, twelve million dollars' worth of jewelry, completely surrounded by people with weapons who don't want you to get your hands on it. From this idea today—blow up something a little farther out of town as a distraction—I can see you guys like to be gaudy. That's fine, fires and explosions have their place, but I think you mean to be gaudy in Palm Beach, and it won't work out for you any better than it did for the movie stars."

Carlson wanted to say something, but Parker held up his hand. "Don't tell me," he said. "I'm not in this, so I don't want to know what the plan is, and you don't *want* me to know."

The three of them looked at one another. Parker watched them, waiting to see what his move should be, but nobody seemed ready to offer any threat. At last, Carlson said, "How's the count coming?"

"Done," Ross said. "Eighty-five and change."

"That's short," Carlson said.

Melander said, "Well, we knew it could be."

Carlson turned back to Parker. "The down payment on the place is a hundred grand. It was higher, but Boyd haggled them down to that, but that's it, rock bottom. Two days from now, this cash here is gonna be an electronic impulse out of a bank in Austin, but it isn't enough. As it is, we're gonna have to borrow black to top it up."

Parker waited.

From the bed, Ross said, "You see how it is. We gotta borrow fifteen, that means we gotta pay back thirty. Man, if we give you your"—he consulted a slip of paper on the bed in front of himself—"twenty-one thousand three hundred nineteen bucks, we're gonna have to borrow almost forty, that's a payback eighty, that begins to cut in."

17

"Also," Carlson said, being very reasonable about it all, "we still need a fourth man, the way we got it set up, so *somebody* has to get that fourth share. That's why we want it to be you."

"No," Parker said.

Again they looked at one another, and again Parker waited for them to make a move, but again it didn't happen. Melander simply said, "He isn't gonna change his mind."

"Well, that's a bitch," Carlson said.

Melander said, "We knew it could happen."

"Still."

Meanwhile, Ross was counting out a little stack of money onto the bed while Carlson got to his feet and crossed over to the closet. Opening the closet door, he pulled out two of the three suitcases in there, leaving Parker's. Ross got off the bed and came over to hand the little stack of cash to Parker, saying, "Sorry it didn't work out. We'll catch up with you later."

Parker looked at the money, and it wasn't enough, nowhere near enough. He said, "What's this?"

"Ten percent," Ross told him. "Just over two grand. When we're done in Palm, you'll get the full amount, so this is like interest on the loan."

"I'm not loaning you anything," Parker said.

Melander and Carlson were stuffing the rest of the cash into the two suitcases. Melander said, "I'm afraid you got to, pal. You don't have a choice, and we don't have a choice."

Ross showed Parker a pistol but didn't exactly

point it at him. "You shouldn't stand up," he said, "and you shouldn't move your hands off the table."

Parker said, "Tom Hurley told me you guys weren't hijackers."

"We aren't hijackers," Ross said with simple sincerity. "You'll get your money. The job goes down two months from now, and then the money's yours. With interest."

Melander said, "Pal, I'm sorry we got to act this way, but what's our choice? We thought you'd come in with us, and then everything'd be fine. I'm sorry you feel the way you do, but there it is."

Carlson said, "You can count on us to pay you. I never stiffed another mechanic in my life."

You're stiffing me now, Parker thought, but what was the point talking?

The three exchanged glances, as though they thought there might be something more to say, and then Melander turned to Parker and spread his hands: "You know where we're going."

"Palm Beach."

"If we were hijackers, we'd kill you now."

The only thing to do, Parker thought, and waited.

Carlson said, "But that isn't our style."

Then you're dead, Parker thought, and waited.

Melander said, "It's just, we'd like you to stay at home the next couple months. We'll phone you sometimes, we'd like to know you're there."

Parker shrugged. There was nothing to say to these people.

Apparently, they now themselves thought they'd

said enough. They moved toward the door, Ross putting the pistol away, and left, not looking back at him.

Parker sat there, hands palm-down on the table, little stack of bills between his hands. His money was gone, about to become an electronic impulse in Texas. This wasn't what it was supposed to be, and it wasn't what it was going to be.

He got to his feet, and crossed to the phone, and called Claire, at the house up in New Jersey. When she answered, without identifying himself he said, "You remember that hotel with the shark scare," meaning a place they'd stayed once in Miami Beach.

"Yes."

"Go there for a couple months, I'll call you."

"Now?"

"You can wait a couple days, till the phone rings, but don't answer," he said, and hung up.

5

He was starting from Evansville, and he had two months to get to Palm Beach. In that time, there would be preparations to make, and preparations cost money. So what he had to do, most of the time, for the next month and a half, was collect money.

Cash is harder to find than it used to be. There are no cash payrolls. Stadium box offices, travel agents, department stores, all deal mostly in credit cards. An armored car can't be taken down by one man working alone. A bank can be taken by a single-O, but all he gets is what's in one teller's cage, which isn't enough for the risk. So it's hard to find cash, in useful amounts. But it isn't impossible.

What he had, including the "interest" his three former partners had given him, was a little over three thousand dollars in cash. The car he was driving, a tan Ford Taurus with Oklahoma plates, was clean enough for a traffic stop, not clean enough for an in-depth study of the paperwork. Clipped under the dash of the Taurus, to the right of the steering wheel column, was a .38 Special Colt Cobra, while under his shirt on the left side, in a narrow suede holster, was a Hi-Standard snub-nose Sentinel .22, useless unless the target is within arm's reach. He also had a few changes of clothing of utilitarian type, to make him look like somebody who works with his hands, and that was it.

What he needed first was better guns, then more money, then better clothing and luggage, then better wheels. He needed to change his appearance, too, not for the three guys he was going to kill but for the Palm Beach police; he needed to be somebody who wouldn't make the law look twice.

Melander had paid for this motel room with a credit card that would probably self-destruct by to-morrow, so the first thing to do was get out of here. Parker carried his bag, lighter than it should have been, out to the Taurus. Five minutes later he was on Interstate 164, headed south into Kentucky.

Throughout the South, there are more gun stores out along the state highways than there are in down-towns or shopping malls, and there's a number of reasons for that. The stores need good parking areas, they don't want to have to deal with antsy neighbors or troublesome landlords or the wrong kind of pedestrian traffic, and most of their customers are rural rather than urban.

So the stores are in the country, but they aren't countrified. They have first-rate security, with solid locks, burglar alarms wired to the nearest state police barracks, shatterproof glass in their display windows, iron bars, and some even have motion sensors.

Parker chose a place called "A-Betta-Deala—GUNS," mostly because it didn't have a dog. It was a broad one-story building beside a state road in central Kentucky, with its name in red letters on a huge white sign on the roof. Flanking the barred and gated double front doors were two wide display windows on either side, three of them featuring rifles and shotguns, the fourth showing handguns.

Two and a quarter miles to the south of the gun shop was the garage and storage lot of the County Highway Department, and four miles beyond that was the nearest state police barracks. Parker left the Taurus at the side of A-Betta-Deala at quarter after three in the morning, where it wouldn't be readily noticed from the road. Then he walked the two and a quarter miles south along the hilly, curvy road through mostly scrub forest. The four times he saw headlights coming, he stepped off the road into the trees until the vehicle went past.

There was much less security at the Highway Department garage; just a bolted chain to keep closed the two sides of the chain-link gate. First putting on the surgical gloves, Parker climbed over the gate and found his way in the darkness to a yellow Caterpillar backhoe with a four-foot-wide bucket. Briefly using his pencil flash, he found the number painted on the side of the cab, then went over to the garage. The side door had a simple lock and no alarm system; he went through it, and used the pencil flash to find the locked plywood cabinet on the wall where the keys were kept. A nearby shovel made a good lever; he popped the cabinet door open and found the back-hoe key. He also picked up a yellow hard hat to wear, to look legitimate, then went back outside.

The backhoe was loud but powerful. He had to back it out of its parking space, and it went *ping ping ping* until he shifted into Drive. Then he swung it around, extended the bucket, rotated it so the open part was facing rearward, and drove it through the locked gate.

The machine's top speed was around twenty miles an hour, and it didn't like to do that much on curves. It took eleven minutes to drive back north to A-Betta-Deala. In that time, one pickup passed, headed south, loud country music trailing from its open windows.

There were no headlights visible up or down the road when Parker reached the gun shop. Without pausing, he angled the bucket with the maw forward and down, then drove directly into the window displaying the handguns. He rotated the bucket, scooping up the window and everything in it, then backed away from the building while the backhoe pinged some more. Clear of the building, which was now screaming a high-pitched alarm wail, he rotated the bucket to spill everything onto the blacktop parking lot, then shut off the backhoe's motor, took off the hard hat, climbed down from the cab, and picked through the rubble, shining the pencil flash. He chose four pistols, went away to the Taurus, put the handguns under a motel blanket on the back seat, stripped off the gloves, and drove north, away from the gun shop, the Highway Department garage, and the state police.

6

Six days later, in Nashville, at eight-thirty in the morning, Parker sat in the Taurus on Orange Street, across the way and up the block from AAAAcme Check Cashing. The place wasn't open yet, so all that showed on the ground floor of the narrow three-story building, one of a row of similar structures along here, was the gray metal of the articulated grille that was drawn down over the facade at night. Once that was raised, the storefront was merely a small-windowed metal door in the middle of a brick wall, with a small wide window high on each side, both windows containing red neon signs that said "Checks Cashed."

This was Parker's fourth morning here, and he now was sure of AAAAcme's opening routine. The business hours of the place were nine A.M. to six P.M., Monday through Saturday. At about eight forty-five

26

every morning, a red Jeep Cherokee would pull up to the store with two men in the front seat. The driver, a bulky guy in a windbreaker no matter how warm the weather, suggesting a bulletproof vest underneath, would get out of the Cherokee, look carefully around, and cross to unlock and lift the metal grille. Then he'd unlock and open the front door, and stand holding it open, looking up and down the street. The other man, also bulky and in a windbreaker, would get out of the Jeep, open its rear door, take out two heavy metal boxes with metal handles on the tops, and trudge them across the sidewalk and into the store. The first man would let the door close, then go back to the Jeep, shut the rear door his partner had left open, and drive half a block to a private parking lot reserved for the bailsmen, pawnshop owners, used musical instrument dealers, liquor store owners, dentists, and passport photographers who ran businesses in the neighborhood. After parking the Jeep in its labeled spot, he'd walk back to the store, knock, and be let in. Fifteen minutes later they'd open for business.

This was more of a late-night than an early-morning neighborhood. There was almost no traffic at this time of day, rarely a pedestrian until midmorning. The three days Parker'd watched, AAAAcme hadn't had a customer before nine-thirty, so their opening time must be merely a long-standing habit.

This morning, the routine was the same as ever. Seeing the Cherokee approach in his rearview mirror, Parker got out of the Taurus, made a show of

27

locking it, and walked down the street toward
AAAAcme. The Cherokee passed him and stopped at
the curb, and he walked by between Cherokee and
storefront. He continued to walk, pacing himself to
the normal speed of their movements behind him,
and the Cherokee passed him again just before he
got to the entrance of the parking lot.

Today he was dressed in a gray sweatshirt over
black chinos. The Sentinel was in the right pants
pocket, and a Colt .45 from Kentucky was tucked into
the front of the chinos under the sweatshirt. Turning
in at the entrance to the parking lot, he put his hand
in his right pocket.

The driver was getting out of the Cherokee. He
gave Parker an incurious look, turned to lock the
Cherokee, and Parker stepped rapidly toward him,
taking the Sentinel out of his pocket, holding it
straight-armed in front of himself, aiming as he
moved. He fired once, and the .22 cartridge
punched through the meat of the driver's left leg,
halfway between knee and hip, then went on to crack
into the door panel of the Cherokee, leaving a
starred black dent.

The driver sagged, astonished, falling against
the Cherokee, staring over his shoulder at Parker:
"What? What?"

Parker stepped very close, showing him the Sentinel. "I shot you," he said. "The vest doesn't cover
the leg. It doesn't cover the eye, either. You want one
in the eye?"

"Who the fuck are *you*?" The driver was in shock,

the blood drained from his face. He pawed at his left leg.

Parker held the Sentinel close to his face. "Answer me."

"What'd I do to you? I don't even know you!"

"I'm robbing you," Parker told him.

"Jesus! You want my—oh, my God!" he cried, staring at his bloodred hand. "For a fucking *wallet*?"

"The store," Parker said. "We'll go there, and we'll go in together."

"My partner—"

"Will do what you tell him. You do right, in a few minutes you're on your way to the hospital. You do wrong, in a few minutes you're on your way to the morgue."

The driver panted, trying to catch up, get his wits about him. "They'll get you, you know," he said.

"So don't sweat it," Parker told him. "It's only money, you're insured, and they'll get me. Let's go."

"I can't walk."

"Then you're no good to me," Parker said, and brought the Sentinel up to his face again.

"I'll try!"

He could walk, with a limp. He kept looking at his red hand, in disbelief. "This is crazy," he said. "You don't just shoot people."

"Yes, I do," Parker said. "What's your name?"

The driver blinked at him, bewildered again. "What?"

"Your name."

"Bancroft. Why, what's—"

"Your first name."

"Jack. John—Jack, people call me Jack."

"Okay, Jack. What's your partner's name?"

"First?"

"First."

"Oliver."

"Ollie?"

"No, he's no Ollie, he's Oliver."

They were approaching the shopfront. Parker said, "Tell him, 'I'm shot, this man helped.' Nothing else. Show him your hand."

Jack nodded. He was panting pretty badly, limping more. His face was still ashen.

As they reached the shopfront, Parker put the Sentinel away and took out the Colt. Jack knocked on the glass in the door, and it was opened partway by Oliver, who stopped abruptly with the door less than a foot open when he saw Parker. He said, "Jack?"

Jack held up his red hand. "I was shot, Oliver, this man helped." He gestured at his leg.

"What?" Oliver looked at Jack's trouser leg, now wet with blood. "Jesus Christ!"

Oliver backed away, and Jack limped in, Parker following, shutting the door behind himself, pushing Jack to one side, showing Oliver the Colt. "Oliver, don't move," he said.

Oliver looked tough and angry, but he hadn't been shot. "You son of a bitch, you—"

He was starting to make a move when Jack called, "He knows about the vests!"

Oliver stopped, frowning at his partner.

"That's right," Parker said. "Your chest is safe from me. Oliver, help Jack to lie on the floor, facedown."

Oliver hesitated. Jack said, "Oliver, I'm hurting. Get this over with, let the cops have it."

Oliver nodded. He told Parker, "They'll get you, you know."

"Jack already told me. Move, Oliver."

Oliver helped Jack to lie facedown on the linoleum floor in front of the counter. The counter was stained wood panel, chest-high, with bulletproof Lucite above and small openings where checks and cash could be passed through. A windowless gray metal door was at one end of the counter, to give access to the rear.

When both men were facedown on the floor, arms behind them, Parker put the Colt away and took from his back pocket a small roll of duct tape. He taped their wrists and ankles, Oliver first, then got Jack's keys from his pocket. He made sure he had the right key to get back into the shop, and left to walk up the block toward the Taurus.

There was still almost no morning traffic around here. Parker drove the Taurus down to AAAAcme, went back inside, and found Oliver and Jack where he'd left them. Jack was breathing like a whale. When he heard Parker move around, he said, "Willya call 911, for chrissake?"

"Somebody will," Parker told him, and went through the metal door to the rear part of the shop, where the two metal cases stood unopened on the

31

floor. He lifted their lids and found the stacks of bills he'd expected.

Looking around, he saw an open safe, which Oliver must have just unlocked for the start of the day. Inside were more stacks of bills, and on top of the safe was a lockable gray canvas money sack. Parker put the bills from the safe in the sack, then opened the cash drawers under this side of the counter, and found more bills. There was change, too, which he left.

The two boxes and the sack were now full. Parker carried everything through to the front door. Oliver kept twisting around to glare at him, but Jack merely lay there, eyes closed, cheek on the floor, mouth open, wheezing.

It took two trips to get everything from the store to the Taurus. Parker propped the store door slightly open, so the first customer would be able to get inside and find Oliver and Jack and make that 911 call, and then, at seven minutes to nine, he drove away, looking for the signs to Interstate 65.

7

In this part of Memphis, integration was complete. There were as many white junkies in this neighborhood as there were black. A number of old-fashioned drunks wandered around here, too, and that's what Parker was passing himself off as.

For nine days, while getting to know this territory, he'd been living in a small bare room in a moth-eaten residence hotel, blending in with the misfits and losers, paying cash, one day at a time. The Taurus, with most of AAAAcme's thirty-seven thousand dollars in the door panels, was stashed in the long-term-parking lot out at Memphis International. Parker kept a bottle of fortified wine sticking out of his hip pocket, and sat around on the sidewalks with the other boozers, though he wasn't the friendly type. He was the sort that kept to himself.

The problem with snooping in a neighborhood

like this is not that people will think you're a heister, but that they'll think you're a cop. Whatever might be going on at higher levels, at the street level the cops around here were on the job, not on the take. The drug dealers had lookouts to warn them when legal trouble was near, and all at once the bazaars would disappear, into alleys and doorways and the back seats of rusted-out cars.

If these people were to decide that Parker was undercover, marking them, they would be determined not to let him live. But he needed to be curious, he needed to trail them, identify them, he needed to follow the money.

It was the scarcity of cash again. AAAAcme had been fine, very easy, but he couldn't keep doing that. If he cut a swath of check-cashing heists across the Southeast, the law would scoop him up before he had anywhere near the amount of money he needed. Every job had to be different, in order to lay no trails, leave no patterns. He didn't want anybody to even think there might be one man out there, doing his work, aiming at something.

So here he was, living on the street in Memphis, letting his beard grow, looking and acting like a stumblebum drunk. It was drug money he wanted now. The dealers are swimming in cash; they concentrate it on and around their persons. But they're constantly getting ripped off, sometimes killed, because that much cash attracts attention, and because everybody knows a robbed drug dealer isn't going to complain to the law. So they're not easy to get at.

On these streets, it seemed as though there were as many dealers as users, and while the dealers were mostly young and combined the cocky with the furtive, the users came in all kinds, from twitching hobos handing over wrinkled dollar bills they've just panhandled to men in suits driving into the neighborhood in Lotuses and Lexuses, pausing for a conversation out a window and an exchange of package for cash.

But it wasn't the street dealers Parker was interested in, not money at that level. What he wanted was higher.

The last nine days, he'd started to work out the delivery system. There were two cars he'd marked, one a black TransAm with fire streaks painted on the hood, the other a silver Blazer with Yosemite Sam brandishing his revolvers on the spare wheel cover. Each would come around two or three times a night, starting and stopping, and the dealers would come out of their holes, and this time the exchange of package for cash would be in reverse: money into the car, package out.

There were at least three people in each of those cars, and Parker was sure there were others as well, scouts who moved ahead of the deliveryman and trailed along behind, looking for law, looking for trouble. Some of the scouts carried walkie-talkies, and all of them were suspicious of every single thing they saw, stumblebum drunks included.

It was the Blazer he started following, on the ninth night, moving away from the area where he'd been hanging out, shuffling six blocks to where he'd seen the Blazer turn onto a side street, then going one block down that side street.

This was a somewhat better neighborhood, but at eleven-thirty at night he didn't look totally out of place. He sat on the sidewalk, back against the front wall of a closed drugstore, and half an hour later the Blazer went by, not moving too fast. Parker watched it, and it ran at least a dozen blocks in a straight line before it went over a small ridge and disappeared.

Different neighborhood; different style from now on. Parker shuffled back to his fleabag, shaved everything but the mustache, which hardly existed yet, and dressed in somewhat better clothes; good enough to hail a cab. Then he packed everything into the small dirty canvas sports bag he'd bought at a pawnshop, left the hotel, walked half a mile, and caught a cab out to Memphis International. Collecting the Taurus, he checked into an airport hotel and paid cash for one night. After room-service dinner and a long shower, he felt more like himself.

The next afternoon, he checked into a motel closer to the city, paying cash for one night. At eleven, he drove into Memphis and parked where he'd last seen the Blazer.

It went by him at twenty after twelve, and kept the straight line for another eight blocks before turning left. When it was out of sight, he started after it, expecting it to be gone and ready to come back to the next post tomorrow night, but when he turned that corner the Blazer was parked at the curb, two and a half blocks away.

He drove slowly by. There was only the driver in the car, and he watched Parker, blank-faced. The Blazer had stopped at a storefront church, its windows blocked with white paper on which was printed outsize biblical quotations. A bright light was over the door, and benches on the sidewalk in front of the windows, and half a dozen hard men on the benches, watching everything; at the moment, watching Parker. He kept going and drove back to the motel.

He set the alarm for five, got up then, moved out of that room, found an all-night diner for breakfast, then drove back to park in the block before the store-front church, which was now dark, the benches in front of it empty.

There was a service at seven-thirty, the congregation mostly old women who had trouble walking, then nothing happened until a little after eleven, when a dark blue Ford Econoline van stopped at the church. A big man got out on the passenger side, looking in every direction at once, and walked into the church.

A minute later he was back out, to open the sliding door of the van. A second man came out after him, carrying two pretty full black trash bags. They were heaved into the van, the second man went back into the church, and the first one slid the door shut. He got in on the passenger side, and the van drove off.

For the next three days, Parker leapfrogged the van, the way he'd done with the Blazer. Every night he checked into a different motel, paying cash for one night. Then, the fourth day, he watched the van drive into the basement garage under a downtown office building. It was a commercial garage, open to the public, so he drove in after it, collecting his ticket at the barrier, seeing the van stopped near the elevators. When he drove by, the passenger was on a cell phone. So these people didn't carry the cash up; someone up there would come down and get it. Probably in something more upscale than trash bags.

There were no parking places free on the first level. He spiraled down to the second, found a spot, left the Taurus, and went over to take the elevator up to the lobby. He stood there by the sidewall, as though waiting for someone, and watched the display lights on the elevator bank. Three elevators were going up. None went to the first parking level for the next five minutes, so the exchange had already been made while he was parking the Taurus. He took the elevator down to the first level himself, and the van was gone. He walked on down to the Taurus.

The next day, he was there early, standing on the sidewalk in front of the building when the van drove in. He walked into the lobby, waited there, and in a minute saw an elevator descend to the first parking level. It held there for a minute while Parker crossed to the elevators and pushed UP.

The elevator arrived, and Parker boarded. Already in there were two white men in suits and a large black wheeled suitcase. The 9 button was lit; Parker pushed 11.

As they rode up, he watched the numbers light above the door. When 7 came on, he took out the Sentinel and shot the nearer man in the arm, then pushed him into the other. "It isn't your money," he said, holding the gun high for them to see, and they stared at him, shocked, too startled to know what to do, both of them still in the process of realizing that one of them had been shot.

Parker waited for the door to slide open at 9. If they had a third guy up here, in the hall, he'd have no choice but to kill them, but he'd prefer not to. Death draws more police heat than wounding.

The ninth-floor hall was empty. Parker pushed DOOR CLOSE, and the unwounded man said, "Do you know who owns this money?"

"Me," Parker said.

The man said, "They'll stuff your nuts in your mouth, and they'll make you watch your children die."

"I can hardly wait," Parker said, and the door opened at 11. "Bring that," he said, gesturing with the Sentinel at the wheeled suitcase.

They came out into the hall, the wounded one holding his arm and watching Parker with a wary look, the other one pulling the suitcase and watching for his chance to make a move.

The hall was empty. A sign said the stairs were to the left. Parker said, "You know I don't want to kill you, or you'd be dead already, but you know I will if I have to. You both have pieces under your coats, and you'll leave them there. Let's walk to the stairs."

They walked to the stairs. A sign on the door there said "No Reentry." In checking the building this morning, Parker had noticed that security arrangement. In case of fire, people could get to the staircase on every floor of the building, but only the door at the lobby level would open from the staircase side.

He'd also looked at the company names on the building directory in the lobby, and Vestro Financial Services on 9 was one of the three outfits that had seemed likely. "You'll get back to Vestro in a little while," he told them, "with a story to tell. Leave the case in the doorway."

They did, propping the door partly open, and the three of them stood close on the concrete landing. The stairwell was bright yellow and had an echoing quality.

Parker took a pair of shoelaces from his pocket, still in their paper band, and gave them to the un-wounded one, saying, "Use one to tie your pal's thumbs together. Behind him."

The wounded one said, "Man, don't do that. I can't move this thing."

"He'll help you," Parker said.

The other one hefted the shoelaces on his palm. "You can still walk away from this," he said.

"I'm in a hurry," Parker told him. "Do I have to do this the very fast way?"

The guy shrugged and said, "Sorry about this, Artie."

"Oh, shit," Artie said, and hissed through his teeth when the other one moved his arm.

Parker watched, and the unwounded one tied the knot well enough. Then he turned to Parker and said, "I suppose you want this one back." He extended the shoelace, but it dropped through his fingers.

He'd been expecting Parker to be distracted by that, as his hand darted in under his jacket, but Parker was not; he stepped forward and shot him in the gut, just above the belt buckle.

The man grunted, folding in on himself, the revolver coming in slow motion out from inside the jacket. Parker plucked it from his hand and pushed his chest; as the man toppled backward down the stairs, he turned to Artie and said, "That makes it easier."

"*I* didn't do anything! *I'm* no trouble!"

Parker put his new revolver on top of the suitcase, reached under Artie's jacket, and found its twin. He tucked both guns under his belt, beneath his shirt, and put the Sentinel back into its holster.

Artie watched him, fearful but not pleading. Parker turned away from him, wheeled the suitcase back out to the hall, and the No Reentry door snicked shut behind him.

8

When he rented the post office box in Pasadena, an industrial suburb southeast of Houston near NASA's manned space center at Clear Lake, Parker used the name Charles O. St. Ignatius. He paid for the first six months and pocketed the small flat key. Then he drove into Houston, where he bought the black suit and the clerical collar he wore when he went to the banks.

"We've started a fund drive at our church," he told the first banker. "We are in desperate need of a new roof."

The banker didn't yet know if he was about to be hit up for the fund drive, so his expression was agreeable but noncommittal. "That's too bad, Father," he said.

"The Lord has seen fit to give us three near-misses

the last several years," Parker told him. "Two hurricanes and a tornado, all just passed us by."

"Lucky."

"God's will. But the effect has been to loosen the roof and make it unstable."

"Too bad."

"Our fund drive is doing very well," Parker told him, and the banker smiled, knowing he was off the hook. "Well enough," Parker went on, "so we'll need to open a bank account, just temporarily, until we raise enough money for the repairs."

"Of course."

Parker pulled out the two white legal envelopes stuffed with cash. "I believe this is four thousand two hundred dollars," he said. "Is cash all right? That's the way the donations come to us."

"Of course," the banker said. "Cash is fine." And under five thousand dollars meant that none of it would be reported to the Feds.

Parker handed over the envelopes, and the banker briskly counted the bills: "Four thousand two hundred fifty dollars," he said.

"Thank you," Parker said.

There was a form to be filled out: "In what name do you want the account?"

"Church of St. Ignatius. No, wait," Parker said, "that's too long. Signing the checks . . ."

The banker smiled in sympathy. "Just St. Ignatius?"

"All right," Parker said. "No, make it C. O. Ignatius, that's the same as 'Church of.'"

"And the address?"

"We've opened a post office box for donations, so let's use that."

"Fine."

A little more paperwork, and Parker was given a temporary checkbook and deposit slips. "My deposits will be in cash, of course," he said.

"We recommend you don't mail cash."

"No, I'll bring it in."

"Fine," the banker said, and they shook hands, and Parker went on to the next bank.

That day, he opened accounts in nine Houston banks, never going to more than one branch of the same firm. When he was finished, thirty-eight thousand dollars was now in the banking system, no longer cash, with nearly eighty thousand still in the side panels of the Taurus.

After the last bank, he drove on down to Galveston and spent the night in a motel with no view of the Gulf. In the morning, he rented a post office box under the name Charles Willis, for which he carried enough ID for any normal business scrutiny, then went to a bank not related to any of the ones he'd used in Houston. As Charles Willis, and using checks from two different St. Ignatius accounts, he opened a checking account with fifteen hundred dollars and a money market account with four thousand, giving the post office box in Galveston as his address. Then he took the free ferry over to Bolivar Peninsula and headed east.

9

The six theaters at the Parish-Plex out St. Charles Avenue had a total seating capacity of nine hundred fifty, ranging from the largest, two hundred sixty-five, where the latest Hollywood blockbusters showed, to the smallest, seventy-five, where art films from Europe alternated with kung fu movies from Hong Kong. When Parker put down his eight dollars for the final screening of *Drums and Trumpets* on Sunday night, it was the fourth time he'd paid his way into this building this week; it would be the last.

Three runs per movie Friday night, five on Saturday, and five on Sunday. First thing Monday morning, the weekend's take would be delivered to the bank, but right now it was still in the safe in the manager's office. The entire multiplex had run at just under eighty percent capacity this weekend, which meant that, once Parker's eight dollars and the rest of the final intake were added, there would be just under seventy-eight thousand dollars in the safe, which was opened only when the cashier brought her money tray up from the box office.

The first time he'd come here, Parker had watched how the system worked for moving the money. When the box office closed, the cashier brought that low flat open tray full of cash upstairs to the manager's office. The manager then closed and locked the door, and about five minutes later she unlocked and opened it again; that would be the time the safe in there stood open. Tomorrow, the cashier would bring starter cash for change back down to the box office in that metal tray.

His second visit, coming to an early show, Parker had waited until the manager left on one of her rounds, then tried the four keys he'd brought with him against the lock in the office door and found the one that worked. The third time, he'd watched the ticket-taker at the door, the only other employee in here except for the concession-stand girl. He was a college kid in a maroon and gray uniform; what did he do when the money was in motion?

Nothing, or nothing that mattered. Once the box office closed, the kid crossed the lobby, went through an Employees Only door and down a flight of stairs to change out of his uniform. So the cashier and the manager were all he had to think about.

Tonight, he stood looking at a poster for a coming attraction, mounted on the wall down the corridor from the manager's office. He read the names and looked at the colored drawing of an exploding train going over a cliff, as the cashier went by behind him, carrying the metal tray. Farther down the hall, the manager stood in the open doorway. She and the cashier had been doing this routine for years. Neither of them was wary, neither of them looked at the customer reading the poster. The cashier went into the office, the manager shut the door, and Parker heard the sound of the lock as it clicked shut.

He waited just over a minute, then slipped on the surgical gloves and moved quickly down the hall. The key was in his right hand, the Sentinel in his left. He opened the door with one quick movement, stepped into the office, and shut the door.

The manager was on one knee in front of the open black metal box of the safe in the corner behind her desk. The cashier had put the money tray on the manager's desk and was just starting to hand the cash to her. They both had stacks of bills in their hands. They looked over at Parker, and neither of them was yet alarmed, just startled that somebody had come through that door.

The manager's name was on a brass plate on her desk. Stepping forward, showing the Sentinel, Parker said, "Gladys, keep that money in your hands. Turn toward me. Turn toward me!" He didn't want her thinking about hurriedly slamming shut the safe.

Gladys merely gaped, thinking about nothing at all yet, but the cashier, a short stocky round-faced woman, stared at the gun in openmouthed shock, then sagged against the desk, the stacks of bills falling from her fingers. Her face paled, sweat beaded on her forehead, and her eyes glazed.

Parker said, "Gladys! Don't let her fall!"

Gladys finally got her wits about her. Scrambling to her feet, tossing onto the desk the money she'd been holding, she leaned toward the cashier, stretching out an arm while she snapped at Parker in a quick harsh voice, "Put that gun away! Don't you know what you're *doing*?"

A short green vinyl sofa stood against the sidewall. Parker said, "Come on, Gladys, help her to the sofa."

Gladys had to come around the desk to reach the cashier, but she still glared at Parker. "She's from Guatemala," she said, as though that explained everything. "She saw . . ."

The cashier was moaning now, sliding down the desk, the strength giving out in her legs. Parker said, "Get her to the sofa, Gladys, and she won't have to look at the gun."

"Maria," Gladys murmured, helping the other woman, moving her with difficulty away from the desk and over toward the sofa. "Come on, Maria, he won't do anything, it's all right."

That's right, Parker wouldn't be doing anything, at least with the Sentinel, not this time. He wanted to not use it unless he absolutely had to, because that, too, could become a pattern, a series of robberies that always began with the wounding of one of the victims.

The two women sat on the sofa, Maria collapsed into herself like a car-crash dummy, Gladys hovering next to her, murmuring, then turning to glare again at Parker and say, "Are you *robbing* us? Is that actually what this is? Are you actually *robbing* us?"

"Yes," Parker said, and moved around the desk toward the safe.

"For *money?*" Gladys demanded. "The *trauma* you're giving this poor woman; for *money?*"

"Keep her calm," Parker said, "and nobody's going to get hurt."

He had brought with him a collapsible black vinyl bag with a zipper, inside his shirt at the back. Now he took it out, put the Sentinel handy on the desk, and stuffed cash into the bag. When it was full, he zipped it shut and put the rest of the money in his pockets.

There was one line in here for both phone and fax. He unplugged the line at the wall and at the phone, rolled it up, and pocketed it, then carried the vinyl bag and the Sentinel over to the two women on the sofa. "Gladys," he said.

She looked up at him. She was calmer now, and Maria was getting over her faint. Gladys was ready to stop being angry and start being worried. "You wouldn't dare shoot that," she said. "Not with all the people around."

"Gladys," Parker said, "there's gunshots going off in the movies all around us. I could empty this into you, and nobody'd even look away from the screen."

Gladys blinked, then stared at the gun. She could be seen braving herself to stare at it. Maria moaned again and closed her eyes, but wasn't unconscious.

Parker said, "I'll wait out in the hall for a few min-

49

utes. If you come out too soon, I'll shoot you. You know I will, don't you?"

She looked from the Sentinel to his face. "Yes," she whispered.

"You decide when to come out, Gladys," he told her. "But take your time. Think what a trauma it would be for Maria, to see you lying in a lot of blood."

Gladys swallowed. "I'll take my time," she said.

10

From a pay phone in Houston, Parker called a guy he knew named Mackey and got his girlfriend Brenda. "Ed around?"

"Somewhere," she said. "I don't think he's looking for work."

"I don't have any. What I want is a name."

"Yours or somebody else's?"

"Both," Parker said. "Maybe he could call me at—wait a minute—two o'clock your time."

"You're in a different time?"

"Yes," he said, and gave her the number of another pay phone, backward.

"I'll tell him," she promised. "How've you been keeping yourself?"

"Busy," he said, and hung up, and went away in his dog collar to make today's cash deposits into his nine bank accounts, and then shift more of that money into the accounts in Galveston.

At three, changed out of the religious clothes, he went to that second pay phone, mounted on a stick to one side of a gas station, by the air hose. He stopped the Taurus in front of the air hose, got out, stepped toward the phone, and it rang.

Ed Mackey sounded chipper, like always. "Brenda says you're looking for a name."

"There was somebody you knew, in Texas or somewhere, could give me a name."

"I know who you mean," Mackey said. "I think he specializes in Spanish names, though, you know? People that wanna bring their money north."

"That doesn't matter," Parker said.

"Okay. He's in Corpus Christi, he's in the phone book there, he calls himself Julius Norte." He pronounced the last name as two syllables: Nor-tay.

"Julius Norte," Parker echoed.

Mackey laughed. "I think maybe his first customer was himself."

"Could you give him a call? Tell him Edward Lynch is coming by."

"Sure. When?"

"Tomorrow sometime," Parker said, and the next day, when he'd finished his bank transactions, he drove south the two hundred miles to Corpus Christi, the southernmost Texan port on the Gulf, nearest to Mexico and South America.

Corpus Christi International Airport is just west of town, down Corn Products Road from Interstate 37, and near there he found tonight's motel. A Southern Bell phone book for the area was in the bottom drawer of the bedside table, and Julius Norte was listed. Parker dialed the number and got an answering machine: "You've reached Poco Repro, nobody in the office right now. Please leave your name and number and we'll get back to you." Then it repeated the same thing in Spanish.

"Edward Lynch," Parker said, and reeled off the phone and room numbers here. Then he went back to the phone book and a local map for restaurants, but hadn't made his decision yet when the phone rang. So Julius Norte was home after all, and screening his calls.

"Yes."

"Mr. Lynch?"

"Yes."

"A friend of yours said you might call."

"Ed Mackey."

"That's the fellow. Where are you?"

"Near the airport."

"You want to come down now?"

"Yes."

"Know where Padre Island Drive is?"

"I can find it."

"Okay," he said, and gave quick precise instructions, and Parker followed them and found himself in a neighborhood that could have been anywhere in the south or west of the United States, from Mobile to Los Angeles: small one-story pastel stucco houses without garages or porches, a little shabby, on small weedy plots of land, with not a tree or a tall bush within miles.

The address Parker wanted was on a corner, with a carport added on the side away from the intersection, and the first surprise was the car in the carport: a gleaming black Infiniti with the vanity plate 1NORTE1. This car cost more than all the other vehicles up and down the block, all combined together.

Parker left the Taurus at the curb and walked up the cracked concrete walk to the small stoop at the front door. Beside the door was a bell button, and above the button on a small hook hung a sign that read "Ring And Walk In."

So now Parker knew a number of things. This was not where Norte lived. He wasn't worried about who might walk through his door. And he was richer than this neighborhood.

He rang the bell, as instructed, and pushed open the door, and stepped directly into what had once been the living room but was now an office, with two desks. The desk to the left rear, facing this way with its side against the wall under the carport window, was a simple gray metal rectangle, and seated at it, just putting down a *fotonovela* to give Parker the double-O, was a guy who looked like a headliner in TV wrestling: long greasy wavy black hair, a neck wider than his forehead, and a black T-shirt form-fitting over a body pumped up with weights. His nose was mashed in, mouth heavy, eyes small and dark under forward-thrusting eyebrows. The look he gave Parker was flat but expectant, like a guard dog's.

The other desk, nearer the door and off to the right, was a much bigger affair, more elaborate, a warm mahogany that took the light just so. A green felt blotting pad, brass desk lamp and gleaming desk set, family photos in leather frames; it had everything.

And the guy seated at the desk had everything, too. He wore a white guayabera shirt that showed off his tan, and his head was topped by a good rug, tannish brown, medium long, nicely waved. Below, his bland nice face had the smooth noncommittal look of much plastic surgery, and when he rose to smile at his visitor it was as though he were holding the smile for somebody else. "Mr. Lynch," he said.

"Mr. Norte," Parker said, and shut the door behind himself.

Norte came around the desk to offer a strong workingman's hand that had not had plastic surgery and so was more truthful about where he came from. Parker shook it, and Norte gestured with it at the brown leather armchair facing the desk. "Sit down, Mr. Lynch," he offered. "Tell me about it. Our friend Ed is well?"

"He didn't say," Parker said.

Norte gave him a quick smile as they both sat, on opposite sides of the desk. The guard dog had gone back to his *fotonovela*. "Down to business, eh?"

"Might as well," Parker said, but took a second to look around. Gray industrial carpeting, a few beige filing cabinets, a closed interior door opposite the entrance. A paper company calendar and a few diplomas on the wall. "You call this place Poco Repro," he said. "What's that?"

"Printing," Norte explained. "Mostly yearbooks, annual reports, banquet programs. More Hispanic than Anglo. But that's not what you want."

"No," Parker agreed. "What I want is ID."

"How good?"

"Real. Good enough to buy a car, take out a loan. I don't need it forever."

Norte nodded. A fat gold pen lay on the green blotter in front of him. He rolled it in his fingers and said, "You must know, real is the most expensive."

"Yes, I know."

"It doesn't matter how long you want it for, you can't sell it back, or even give it back. Once you've got it, it's yours."

Parker shrugged. "Fine."

"Do you care about the backstory?"

"Just so there's no paper out on the name."

"No, of course." Norte considered, looking past Parker at the front window. "The Social Security won't be real," he said. "I can't get a legitimate number that works in their system."

"That should be okay," Parker said.

"I'm thinking of some friends of mine," Norte said, "naturalized citizens. Is that okay?"

"I gotta have a name that looks like me."

"Oh, yes, sure, I know that. You could be Irish, no?"

"I could be."

"Many Irish went to South America," Norte told

him, "in the nineteenth century, did well, the names survive. In Bolivia, other countries, you've got your José Harrigan, your Juan O'Reilly."

"I can't use 'Juan,'" Parker said.

"There are names that cross over," Norte said. "Oscar. Gabriel. Leon. Victor."

"Fine."

"And when would you like this?" Norte asked, but laughed before Parker could say anything and said, "Never mind, that was not a smart question. You want it as soon as you can get it, no?"

"Yes."

"Texas resident?"

"That would be best," Parker said.

"And easiest for me. So you want a driver's license and a birth certificate. Do you need a passport?"

"No."

"Now you surprise me," Norte admitted. "Most people, that's the first thing they want."

"My troubles are domestic," Parker told him.

Norte laughed. "All right, Mr. Lynch," he said, "you can stop being Mr. Lynch, I think, in three days' time. Is that all right?"

"That's fine," Parker said.

Norte said, "But then again, you haven't been Mr. Lynch all that long, have you? Never mind, that wasn't a question. You didn't bring a photo, did you?"

"No."

"We can do that here," Norte assured him. "The other thing is money."

"I know."

"Driver's license, birth certificate, both with legitimate sources. Ten thousand. Cash, of course."

"I like cash," Parker said.

"There's so little of it around these days," Norte said. "That would be in advance. Sorry, but it's best that way."

Parker said, "Will you be here in half an hour?"

"If you intend to be," Norte told him.

Parker got to his feet. "Nice to meet you, Mr. Norte," he said.

"And you, Mr. Lynch."

11

When Parker went back to Norte's office half an hour later, he'd made two stops, the first at a drugstore where he'd bought reading glasses of the lowest possible magnification, 1.25, and a dark brown eyebrow pencil. The glasses were squarish and black-framed, and the eyebrow pencil would work to emphasize his new mustache. And the second stop he'd made, in the far corner of a supermarket parking lot, had been to open a door panel and remove from inside it ten thousand in cash.

Again he rang the bell and walked in, and again the guard dog looked up from his *fotonovela* to watch Parker cross the room. Norte was on the phone, but he said something quiet in Spanish, hung up, and got smiling to his feet. "Right on time," he said.

He wanted to shake hands again, so Parker shook his hand, then took out the money and placed it on the desk. Norte smiled at it. "You don't mind if I count."

"Go ahead."

Norte did, then said, "Bobby will take your picture."

"Bobby?"

Norte indicated the guard dog. "Roberto," he said. "Not a name you could use."

"No."

Norte spoke to Bobby in Spanish, and the guard dog put down his *fotonovela* and stood. Norte said to Parker, "You go with Bobby."

Parker went with Bobby, through the door at the back of the room into what still was a kitchen, though not many meals would be made here. Bedrooms and a bathroom were off the kitchen to the right and rear.

A camera was set up on a tall tripod at head height, facing a blank wall. Bobby, moving toward the camera, made a shooing gesture for Parker to stand by the wall. When Parker went over there, he saw a pair of white footprints painted on the floor and stood on them.

Bobby was efficient, if silent. He moved his head to show Parker how to pose, then quickly took three shots. Still saying nothing, he led Parker back to the other room.

The money was gone from the desk, and Norte was standing beside it, smiling farewell. "Phone me Friday afternoon," he said. "It should be ready by then."

"Good," Parker said, and left, and drove back to

the motel. Later, after dinner, he put on black clothing, took his b&e tools out from under the trunk bed in the Taurus, and drove south again, one hundred fifty miles almost to the border, turning east at Harlingen toward South Padre Island, where the rich boaters keep their country villas and retirement homes.

Bay View, Laguna Vista, Port Isabel; this is where the Gulf Intracoastal Waterway begins, where the rich sea-loving Texans are based, alternating between agreeable "cottages" and even more agreeable yachts, moored just at the end of the lawn. In the evenings, they visit one another, play bridge, drink, gossip, plan excursions across the Gulf to the islands of the Caribbean. Half the houses are full of light, warmth, good cheer; the other half are empty.

A little after nine in the evening, Parker left the Taurus in the parking lot of a chain drugstore that wouldn't close till midnight. He left the parking lot over a chain-link fence at the back, and kept to the rear of houses, moving as far as possible from the lit-up noisy ones, crossing only side streets and only at their darkest points. This area was patrolled almost as heavily as Palm Beach, but he was keeping himself dark and silent.

All of the houses along the Waterway are equipped with alarm systems; enter through any door or window, and if the alarm is not switched off at the control pad within forty-five seconds it will signal both the town police and the security service. But where is the control pad to be found? In every house, it is just

61

inside, next to the door nearest to where the car is parked. It was never hard to figure out which door that was.

In the next hour and a half, Parker went into nine houses, and the method was always the same. Interior pockets in the back of his coat carried his tools, which included a telephone handset with alligator clips, a special one used by telephone company repairmen to check lines. With this, he could attach to the house's phone line outdoors, where it came in from the pole, and call that line. He could always hear it ring, inside the house. If the answering machine picked up, or there was no answer after ten rings, and no dog barked, it was his. He'd go to the door nearest where the car would normally be parked and use his small pry bar to pop it.

Inside, on the wall, its red light lit, would be the alarm control pad. He never needed the full forty-five seconds to short-circuit and disarm it. Then he'd move through the house, looking only for cash. He had to leave behind hundreds of thousands of dollars' worth of jewelry, bonds, paintings, cameras, watches, and all the other toys of the leisured rich, but it didn't matter: there was always cash. There was often a wall safe, which he would find by lifting pictures along the way and get into with hammer and chisel, and the wall safes always produced bundles of cash, often still in the paper band from the bank.

Nine houses, a little over a hundred twenty thousand dollars. Finished, he skirted the areas he'd already been through, made his way back to the drugstore fifteen minutes before it would close, and drove back north to Corpus Christi.

Tomorrow, he'd have more money for the banks in Houston.

12

On Friday, from a different motel in Corpus Christi, Parker phoned Norte, got the Poco Repro machine, left a message, and Norte phoned right back: "We're ready, Mr. Lynch," he said.

"I'll come right down," Parker told him, and drove down to Norte's place, but when he turned the corner a black Chevy Blazer was parked in front of the house, with white exhaust visible at the tailpipe. Parker decided not to stop, but drove on by, and saw the driver alone in the Blazer, a chunky man in a white dress shirt, with the pie face and thick black hair of the Mayan Indian. He sat facing front, hands on the steering wheel, waiting, patient.

Another customer was with Norte. Parker drove on down to the next corner and went around it. He didn't want Norte's other customers to meet him, and they probably didn't want him to meet them.

He spent ten minutes driving around the neighborhood before going back to Norte's house again, to see the Blazer still there. But this time its engine was off and the driver was gone.

Parker slowed, peering at the house. The "Ring Bell And Walk In" sign, which had been there ten minutes ago, was gone now from its hook above the bell button.

Something wrong. Parker drove three-quarters of the way around the block, parked, and walked on to the house.

Blazer still there, sign still gone. No one visible in the windows. He walked up to the house and around it to the left to the carport. The Infiniti was there, as before. There was just enough room between the car and the house to slide down there and look through the high window over Bobby's desk.

Norte was at his own elegant desk, on the phone. Bobby stood in the middle of the room, an automatic loose in his hand. Three men lay facedown on the floor, wrists and ankles and mouths swathed in duct tape. One of them was the Mayan driver.

The thing to do was go away somewhere and phone. Parker moved back from the window, sidled past the Infiniti, and when he got to the front corner of the house Bobby was there, the automatic pointed at Parker's chest. With his other hand he gestured: *Come with me.*

Parker shrugged. He walked past Bobby and around to the front door and in, Bobby trailing after him.

Norte was off the phone now, standing behind his desk, looking aggravated. "Bad timing, Mr. Lynch," he said.

"Hand me the papers and I'll go," Parker told him.

Two of the men, not the driver, had twisted around to stare up at Parker, not as though he might help but as though he might be more trouble. Norte, with a sad smile and a harried look, shook his head. "I'm sorry," he said. "You see the situation here, no?"

"Dissatisfied customers," Parker suggested.

But Norte shook that away. "No, I don't have dissatisfied customers. What I got, I got a customer doesn't want anybody alive that knows who he is now and what he looks like now. That fuckhead sent these fuckheads to kill Bobby and me."

"He sent the wrong fuckheads," Parker said.

"So now I gotta take *them* down," Norte said with a disgusted gesture at the men on the floor, "and I gotta take their boss down, because I don't need this shit."

"It's not my fight," Parker said. "Just give me the papers and I'll go."

"I wish I could," Norte said, and he sounded as though he meant it. "But you're a witness here, no?"

"I don't witness things," Parker told him.

Norte didn't like it. He chewed the inside of his cheek, and then he said, "I tell you what. When I get this shit straightened out here, I'll call Ed Mackey, tell him the situation, see what he thinks I should do."

Parker watched him.

Norte tried a smile while still chewing his cheek. He said, "That'll work, no? Ed Mackey knows you."

"He knows me."

"In the meantime," Norte said, "just lie down on the floor here."

"Sure," Parker said, and as he bent forward he reached inside his shirt. He pivoted the holster down, lifted his left arm, and fired through his shirt.

The bullet hit Bobby somewhere, it didn't matter where. It wouldn't stop him, only confuse him for a second; long enough, maybe, for Parker to drop to his knees, turning, pulling the Sentinel out, hearing the big boom of the automatic bounce in this enclosed room, knowing the bullet had gone over his head. He thrust his arm out as Bobby adjusted his aim, and shot the guard dog in the face.

That still didn't finish him, but it made him drop the automatic as he whipped both hands up to his ruined face. He tottered there as Parker dropped the Sentinel, grabbed the automatic, and lunged to his feet.

Norte was pulling a blunt revolver out of a desk drawer, ducking down low behind his desk, calling, "Drop that!"

"Fuck you," Parker said, and pulled Bobby in front of himself to take Norte's first three shots. Now he held the dead Bobby up in front of himself and moved forward toward the desk as Norte, still hidden behind it, called, "All right! I'm done!"

"Put the gun on the desk," Parker told him.

67

Norte stayed out of sight behind the desk. "We don't have to kill each other," he said.

"We're not gonna kill each other."

"I was worried, I was upset, I was too hasty. Ed Mackey said you were okay, I should've remembered that."

"Put the gun on the desk."

Still he remained out of sight. "People need me," he said. "They won't like it if you take me down. Ed Mackey won't like it."

Parker waited.

"I was wrong," Norte said. "I was too hasty."

Parker waited.

"There's no reason to do anything anymore."

Parker waited.

Norte's hand appeared, with the revolver. He put it on the green blotter and pushed it a little forward.

Parker let Bobby fall, on top of the men on the floor. He went forward and walked around the side of the desk to where Norte crouched there, looking up. Norte, voice shaking a little, said, "You don't need to do a thing. I got your documents, middle drawer. You'll see, they're beautiful."

"Let's see them."

Norte hesitantly rose, then looked at his revolver still on the desk. "Aren't you gonna take that?"

"You intend to reach for it?"

"No!"

"Let's see this ID."

Norte opened the middle drawer, took out a manila envelope, shook two official papers out onto the green blotter. He was careful to keep as far as possible from the revolver. He stepped back to the wall, holding the manila envelope, and gestured for Parker to look them over.

His name was Daniel Parmitt. He'd been born in Quito, Ecuador, of American parents, and the birth certificate was in Spanish. His Texas driver's license showed he lived at an address in San Antonio. The photo on the driver's license, with the glasses and the mustache, made him look less hard.

He pocketed both documents, looked around the room. What had he touched? The carpet, Bobby; nothing that would leave prints. "Come here," he said.

Norte didn't move. His hands fidgeted with the manila envelope the documents had been in as he said, "It's a misunderstanding, it's all over. Bobby and me, we were gonna take these shits away, not mess up the office, then all of a sudden we got you here—it was too much goin on, I got too hasty."

"Come here," Parker said.

It finally occurred to Norte that he was still alive and that he needn't be. With small steps, he came forward to the desk and Parker took the manila envelope out of his hands. "Pick up the gun," he said.

"No!"

Parker held the automatic leveled at Norte's forehead. "You aren't gonna point it at me," he said. "You're gonna finish those three."

"Here? We didn't want to—"

69

"Bobby's messing your rug already. The other way is, I do you and I do them and I go."

"But what—"

"Ed says you're useful. I say you're too jumpy to be reliable, but you do good work. If you make it possible, I'll help you stay alive. Pick up the gun."

"And, and kill them?"

"That's what it's for," Parker said.

Norte stared down at the three men. The driver was still stoic, but the other two were now staring up at Norte, hoping something different was going to happen now.

No. Abruptly, as though to get it over before he had to think about it, Norte grabbed up the revolver, bent over them, and shot each one in the head. The carpet would have to be replaced for sure.

"Keep shooting," Parker said.

Norte grimaced at him. "They're dead. Believe me, they're dead."

"Keep shooting."

Norte looked down at the bodies and fired at random into their backs. One, two, *click;* the revolver was empty.

Parker held out the manila envelope. "Put it in here."

Norte frowned, studying Parker's face. "You want a hold over me."

"You make all this go away, what hold? All I need is, *I* was never here."

Norte managed a twisted smile. "Oh, if only that could be true, no?"

"We can make it true. Put the gun in here."

Norte shrugged and reached forward to slide the revolver into the envelope.

Parker said, "Stand back over there by the wall."

Obediently, Norte moved back to where he'd stood before. He kept his arms at his sides, palms forward, to show he wasn't going to try anything, but Parker already knew that.

Parker put the envelope, bulging and heavy with the revolver, on the green blotter. He went around the desk, found his Sentinel near Bobby's feet, and put it back in its holster. Then he picked up the envelope. Automatic in his right hand, envelope in his left, he backed to the door, as Norte looked around at the mess he had to clean up. His face had gone through too much surgery to permit it to show his emotions, but they were there in his eyes.

With a little trouble, Parker turned the doorknob with the hand holding the envelope. He stepped outside, let the door snick shut, and put the automatic under his shirt, keeping his hand on it in there, like Napoleon. But, as he walked away, Norte did not come outside. He had enough to think about.

13

Daniel Parmitt's address in San Antonio, according to his driver's license, was an office building downtown; nobody lived there.

Parker stayed in three motels off Interstate 10 for three nights while setting himself up in town. A real estate agent showed him rental houses, and the second day he found what he needed in Alamo Heights, between McNay Art Museum and Fort Sam Houston National Cemetery. It was a three-bedroom two-story fake-Gothic yellow clapboard house with a turret, set back from a winding, hilly street among modestly upscale houses. Parker knew it was right, but didn't tell the real estate agent; they looked at another four places before he suggested they try again tomorrow.

It was then two-thirty in the afternoon, time enough to get to a bank and open a checking account for Daniel Parmitt, using the address of the house he hadn't rented yet, starting the account with a thirty-eight-hundred-dollar check from Charles O. St. Ignatius in Houston and a forty-two-hundred-dollar wire transfer from Charles Willis's money market account in Galveston, so the money would be available at once. From there he went to the post office and the Department of Motor Vehicles, putting in a change of address from the office building to the new house at both.

Next day, he said to the real estate agent, "Let's look at that yellow house again."

"I *thought* you'd like it," she said, and this time he did.

Daniel Parmitt signed a two-year lease and left a check for two months' rent plus one month deposit. Parker bought a sleeping bag, the only furnishing he'd need in the house, and settled down to wait.

What he mostly had to do now was move money through his bank accounts, gradually cleaning out all the St. Ignatius accounts in Houston, emptying the two accounts Charles Willis had in Galveston, and concentrating the money into Parmitt's checking and money market accounts in San Antonio.

While doing that, he also went shopping. Daniel Parmitt was a rich Texan with a background in the oil business, a man who may have worked at some time in his life but happily doesn't have to anymore, and Parker should dress the way Daniel Parmitt should look. He bought casual slacks and blazers, gaudily colored dress shirts with white collars, shoes with tassels or little gold figures attached to the vamp, yachting caps and white golf caps. He also bought obviously expensive luggage to put it all in.

During this time, he waited to see what the Department of Motor Vehicles would do. If Parmitt's license was real, as Norte had promised, the change of address would go through without a hitch, and he'd be safe to show that license anywhere. If Norte had lied, or made a mistake, the request would bounce back to him.

But it didn't. Two weeks into his stay at the turreted yellow house in San Antonio, Daniel Parmitt got his first piece of mail at his new address: his revised driver's license.

His local Jaguar dealer was happy to talk about leases. There was a little frown of doubt when, on the credit application form, he put down that he'd been at his present address for one month, and gave his previous address as Quito, Ecuador, but then he said, "I was in the oil business down there," and it was all right. Texans understand the oil business.

Six weeks and two days after Melander and Carlson and Ross had made their mistake in Evansville, Daniel Parmitt got behind the wheel of his yellow Jaguar convertible, top down, rear full of luggage, left his yellow home in San Antonio, and drove eastward on Interstate 10. Three days later he'd covered the thousand miles to Jacksonville, Florida, taking his time, not pushing it, and there he turned southward onto Interstate 95. A day and a half later he turned off at Miami.

14

Claire was not in her room. He found her out by the pool in a two-piece red bathing suit, on one of the white chaises there, ignoring the interest she aroused and reading a biography of Aphra Behn.

It had been a while since he had seen her at a different angle like this, coming upon her as though she were a stranger, and it reminded him of the first time they'd met, when he'd opened a hotel room door expecting some flunky driver and had seen this cool and beautiful woman instead. When he told her then he hadn't expected a woman in the job because it was unprofessional she'd said, "It doesn't sound like a very rewarding profession," and already he'd been snagged. Closed off before then, indifferent to the world except as it had to be tamed and manipulated, he hadn't known he could be snagged, but here she was. And here again. Still here.

In his dark blue yachting cap, sunglasses, mustache, pale green blazer, candy-striped dress shirt, white slacks, and tan shoes with tassels, he walked through the sun and the people and the coconut smells of sunblock to sit on the chaise next to her, sideways, to face her. Without looking away from her book, she said, "That's taken."

"By me," he said.

She, too, was in sunglasses, dark green lenses and white plastic frames. She turned her head to give him her cool look through those lenses, then frowned, removed the sunglasses, looked him up and down in astonished distaste, and said, "Good God!"

He grinned. She was the only thing that made him grin. He said, "It works, I guess."

She studied him, detail by detail, then gave him a small quirk of a smile as she said, "This person. Can he be any good in bed?"

"Let's find out," he said.

"Now I remember you," she told him, smiling, and ran her finger along the purplish furrow on his left side, just above the waist, where a bullet once had passed him by, fired by a man named Auguste Menlo, now dead. "My human target."

"I haven't been shot for a long time," he said, and stretched beside her on the bed.

"Not since you met me. I'm good luck for you."

"That must be the reason I'm here," he said, and reached for her again.

He'd been shot eight times, over the years, with puckered reminders still visible on his body, but the only one that showed when he was dressed was the little nick in the lobe of his right ear, as though he'd been docked for branding. A man named Little Bob Negli, who hadn't yet figured out that his Beretta .25 automatic was shooting high and to the right, had made that nick, firing at him from behind. Negli, too, was dead, but Parker was alive, and in the cool dimness in Claire's hotel room he felt that life quicken.

In the morning, she said, "The mustache is wrong."

"Tell me."

"It's a policeman's mustache, too bushy. What you want is a lounge lizard's mustache, smaller, daintier. Think of David Niven or Errol Flynn."

"You do it."

"All right."

They stood in the shower together, she very intent with her nail scissors, and he watched her eyes, how the light took them.

Later he put on his strange clothes, and she watched him, amused. "Is that what you'll wear when you come back?"

"No."

"Don't get shot any more," she said, and kissed him, which covered the fact he didn't have an answer

Richard Stark

for her. But she hadn't asked him any questions, and she still didn't.

At two-thirty that afternoon, in bright sunlight, temperature 76, humidity not too bad, he drove in the yellow Jaguar over the Flagler Memorial Bridge onto Royal Poinciana Way, in Palm Beach.

78

TWO

1

Welcome to the Breakers, sir."

"I have a reservation. The name is Parmitt."

"Yes, sir, here it is. You'll be staying with us three weeks?"

"That's right."

"And what method of pay—oh, I see. We will be billing your bank in San Antonio, is that right?"

"They keep all my money. I'm not permitted to walk around with it myself."

The clerk offered an indulgent smile; he was used to the incompetent rich. "It must take a worry off your mind," he said.

Parker touched the tips of two fingers to his lounge lizard mustache; it felt like half a Velcro strip. "Does it?" he asked, as though the idea of having a worry *on* his mind had never occurred to him. "Yes, I suppose it does," he decided. "In any case, I'm not worried."

"No, sir. If you'd sign here."

Daniel Parmitt.

"Will that be smoking or non, sir?"

"Non."

"And will you be garaging a vehicle with us during your stay, sir?"

"Yes, I left it with the fellow out there. He gave me a—wait, here it is."

"Yes, very good, thank you, sir. You keep this, you'll show it to the doorman whenever you want your car."

Parker held the ticket, frowning at it, then sighed and nodded and put it away in his trouser pocket. "I can do that," he decided.

"And will you be needing assistance with your luggage, sir?"

"The fellow put it on a cart, over there somewhere."

"Very good. Front! Do enjoy your stay with us, Mr. Parmitt."

"I'm sure I will," Parker said, and turned to find a bellboy at his elbow, who wanted to know what room he was in. Parker didn't know until the bellboy helpfully read it aloud for him off the little folder containing his keycard.

"I'll meet you up there, sir, with your luggage."

"Fine. Thank you."

He stood where he was until the clerk said, "The elevators are just over there, sir."

"Thank you."

He rode the elevator up, alone in the car, and strode down the quiet hall to his room. Entering, he faced a wide window, thinly curtained, with the ocean and the bright day visible outside. When he looked at the king-size bed, he thought of Claire, whom he would see again . . . when? In three weeks? Sooner? Never?

A rapping at the door meant the bellboy with the luggage. Parker went through the usual playlet with him, being shown the amenities, the luggage placed just so, lights switched on and off, then the bellboy accepting the rich tip Parker gave him and smiling himself back out the door.

About to start unpacking, Parker caught sight of himself in one of the several mirrors and stopped. He studied himself and knew that what he was doing was the thing to do, the way to be here without being seen, without causing questions to be asked, but still, it felt strange and it looked strange. This person, in these clothes, in this room, on this island.

Well. Whatever tactics he decided on in the next couple of weeks, he knew one thing for certain: he wouldn't be intimidating anybody.

2

"This is my first time in Palm Beach," Parker told the real estate woman, "and I find I'm taking to it quite a bit."

The real estate woman was pleased. A round-faced blonde of about forty, an ex-cheerleader with padding, she wore a beige suit, matching shoes, paler plain blouse, a gold pin of a leaping dolphin on her right breast, and a simple strand of pearls at her throat. She was one of an interchangeable half dozen of such women in this spacious cool office on Worth Avenue, where the only difference was in the color each woman had chosen for today's suit (skirt, not pants); there was peach, there was avocado, there was coconut, there was canary yellow, and there was royal blue. It was a garden of padded real estate women, and how did they decide each morning which one would be Kim, which Susan, which Joyce? The one talking with Parker had chosen to be Leslie today.

"Palm Beach isn't for everyone," she said, though still with her welcoming smile. "Those who will find it *the* place in their lives tend to know that right away."

"I don't know as how it could be *the* place for me," Parker told her, leaning into the characterization, knowing he would never be as seamlessly plausible as Melander, talking about the little Mexicans, but thinking he could do it well enough to pass. "I have other places I like," he explained. "South Padre Island. Vail. But Palm Beach has something that appeals to me."

"Of course," she said with that smile. Her teeth were large and white and even.

"To have a place here, oh, for a month a year, January or February, that might not be bad."

She made a note, on the form on which she'd already filled in his particulars: name, home address, bank, staying at the Breakers. She said, "Would you be entertaining?"

"You mean, how big a place would I need. Yes, of course, I'd have guests, I'd want room to spread out."

"Not a condo, then," she said.

He already knew that much about Palm Beach. "Leslie," he said, "the condos aren't Palm Beach. They're south on the island, their own thing, little places for retired accountants. I'd want something— well, you tell me. What's the neighborhood I want?"

She opened a desk drawer, pulled out a map, and laid it in front of him. With a gold pen, she made marks on the upside-down map as she described the territory. "The most sought-after section, of course," she told him, "is what we call between-the-clubs, because *real* Palm Beachers want to belong to both of the important clubs, so to have a place between them is very convenient."

"Sounds good."

"The Everglades Club, at the north, is here on Golf Road. Then the area of County Road and Ocean Boulevard here is the section I'm talking about, down to the Bath and Tennis Club, here where Ocean Boulevard turns inland at the Southern Boulevard Bridge."

"These are all oceanfront?"

"Well, they're both," she said. "Lake Worth runs along here, on the mainland side of the island. Here, just below Bath and Tennis, where Ocean Boulevard curves in away from the sea, we have estates with ocean frontage, but some of them have tunnels under Ocean Boulevard to the beach on Lake Worth, so the property actually extends through from ocean to lake."

"And the lake is more protected than the ocean."

"Exactly." Then she smiled and said, "One of our ladies, some years ago, to keep from being served papers in a divorce, ran through the tunnel to escape. Unfortunately, they were waiting on the other side."

He saw that that was gossip that was supposed to make them more comfortable with one another, and that he was supposed to laugh now, so he laughed and said, "Too many people know about the tunnels, I guess."

"Not that they aren't *secure*," she assured him. "No one you don't want could get in."

"But if you go out," he said, "they'll be waiting for you."

She smiled, a bit doubtfully. "Yes," she said.

"But this area," he said, running his finger along it on the map, "isn't between the clubs, it's south of them."

"But very close," she said. "It would be in the same range."

"And what is that range? What are we talking about along there?"

"*When* something's available, and nothing is at the moment, you could expect to pay fourteen or fifteen."

Parker shook his head, looking solemn. "My bank wouldn't let me do that," he said. "For a month a year? No. I wouldn't even raise the issue."

"Then you're not going to be between the clubs," she said. She was very sympathetic about it.

"I understand that," he assured her. "But there's got to be something that's not all the way up to these places but not all the way down to the condos."

"But with ocean frontage, you mean."

"Naturally." He shrugged. "You don't come to Palm Beach *not* for the water."

"Well, you can go south of Bath and Tennis," she said. "For quite a ways along there, you'll find some *very* nice estates, mostly neo-Regency, on the sea, or some facing it across the road. Of course, the farther

85

south you go, the closer you are to the condos." As though to say, the closer you are to the Minotaur.

"I tell you what," he said. "Take half an hour, show me these neighborhoods, give me some idea what's out there."

"That's a good idea," she agreed, and pulled her purse out of the bottom drawer of her desk. "We'll take my car."

"Fine."

It took more than half an hour; they spent almost two hours driving up and down the long narrow island in bright sunshine. Her car was a pale blue Lexus, heavily air-conditioned, its back seat full of loose-leaf ledgers and stacks of house-description sheets, many with color photos.

She drove well, but didn't give it much attention; mostly, she talked. She talked about the neighborhoods they were going through, about the history of Palm Beach, the famous people connected with the place, who mostly weren't famous to Parker, and the "style" of the "community." *Style* and *community* were apparently big words around here, but both words, when they were distilled, came down to money.

But not just any money, not for those who wanted to "belong"—another big word that also meant money. Inherited money was best, which almost went without saying, though Leslie did say it, indirectly, more than once. Married money was okay, second best, which was why people here didn't inquire too much into new spouses' pasts. Earned money was barely acceptable, and then only if it acknowledged its inferiority, and absolutely only if it wasn't being earned anymore.

"Donald Trump never fit in here," Leslie said, having pointed out Mar-a-Lago, which for many years had belonged to Mrs. Merriweather Post, who definitively *did* fit in here, and which after her death had been for years a white elephant on the market—nobody's inherited money, no matter how much of it there was, could afford the upkeep of the huge sprawling place—until Trump had grabbed it up, expecting it to be his entrée to Palm Beach, misunderstanding the place, believing Palm Beach was about real estate, like New York, never getting it that Palm Beach was about money you hadn't earned.

"I should be pleased Mr. Trump took over Mar-a-Lago," Leslie said, "I think we should all be pleased, because we certainly didn't want it to turn into Miss Havisham's wedding cake out there, but to be honest with you, I think a place must be just a *little* déclassé if Donald Trump has even heard of it."

Parker let all this wash over him, responding from time to time with his Daniel Parmitt imitation, looking out the windshield at the bright sunny day, looking at the big blocky mansions of the unemployed rich. Neo-Regency style in architecture, when it was pointed out to him, seemed mostly inspired by the Tomb of the Unknown Soldier: molded plaster wreaths on the outside walls, marching balustrades, outsize Grecian urns dotted around like game pieces.

But although Daniel Parmitt was supposedly looking at all this with the eye of someone who just might

want to buy into it, into the whole thing, the property, the *community,* the *style,* in which case Leslie
would be the real estate agent, the mentor, and the
guide, what Parker was looking for was something
else. What he wanted was the house Melander had
bought, partly with Parker's money.

And there it was.

They'd traveled south, out of the commercial part
of town, through between-the-clubs, where the big
houses were mostly hidden behind tall hedges of
ficus and, less successfully, sea grape. They'd driven
on south beyond the Bath and Tennis Club, driving
over the tunnels that let the ocean-facing residents
swim in the lake, then past Mar-a-Lago, and past one
of the very few public beaches on the island, Phipps
Ocean Park, and then more big houses, and in the
driveway of one of them, just barely visible past tow-
ering sea grape and a closed wrought-iron gate,
squatted a Dumpster.

"Work being done there," he said.

"Oh, there's always renovation, here and there,"
she told him. "There's a more than adequate work-
force over in West Palm, and people add things to
their houses constantly. Lately, people have been
putting lots of lights outside, to light up the ocean, so
they can have their view all night long."

"And no burglars," Parker said.

Leslie laughed, dismissing that. "Oh, no, there
aren't any burglars," she said. "Not here."

"The paper says there's burglars."

She was still dismissive. "Oh, every once in a while,

some idiots come up from Miami, but they never last long, and they always get caught. And the city keeps wanting to put some sort of control on the bridges, to get identification on everybody who comes to the island. There's some sort of civil rights problem with the idea, but I really believe they'll figure out how to do it someday. And you know, just here in Palm Beach, we have a sixty-seven-man police force."

Parker had been seeing patrol cars in motion every minute or two since they'd started to drive. "A lot of cops," he said.

"*More* than enough," she assured him. "Crime is not the problem here." Then she giggled and said, "Liver transplants are more the problem than crime in Palm Beach."

"I suppose so," Parker said. "But that place back there got me to thinking. The bank might like it if I found a fixer-upper."

Surprised, she said, "Really?"

"Well, they always talk about value-added, you know," he explained. "God knows I don't want to *work*, I wouldn't even oversee the job, but my man at the bank does like it if I put my money somewhere that it grows itself."

"Oh, I see what you mean. You'd put money into that kind of house, but then when you were finished it would be worth more than you put in."

"That's what they like," Parker said.

"Well, we don't get that sort of thing very much, not around here," she said. "People tend to take care of their places in Palm Beach."

"Oh. That one back there just looked—I suppose they were just renovating."

"No, you have a very good eye," she told him. "That place *was* a wreck. A very sad history. They'd had a fire, and I don't know, it had just been left alone too long."

"But somebody got there before me."

"I believe," she said, remembering, pleased by the memory, "I believe he's also a Texan, like yourself."

Melander and his little Mexicans. "Lucky him," Parker said.

"There's nothing else like that around right now."

"Just a thought," he said.

"You know," she said, "I might still have the sheet on that. I didn't sell it, but—let me pull in at Monegasque."

That was a restaurant, not far ahead, a rare spot on this road where it was possible to pull off to the side. Leslie stopped in front of the place, ignored the valet parkers watching her, and grabbed the stack of house-description sheets from the back seat. She riffled through them and pulled one. "Here it is. You can see the trouble you missed. I don't think fixer-uppers are worth the trouble, frankly."

Here it was. Color photo, taken from an angle to minimize the neglect. Floor plan. Entrances. Description of alarms.

"I'll keep this, if it's okay with you," Parker said.

"Go ahead," she said. "I don't need it. That house is sold."

3

A mile or so south of Melander's house, the private estates began to give way to the hotels: Four Seasons, Hilton, Howard Johnson, all tending down toward the condos. Parker left the Jaguar, top up, in a parking area of the Four Seasons a little after midnight, made his way out to the beach, and walked north. Far ahead, he could see lights along the shore, probably for the nighttime views of the sea Leslie had talked about, but along here the land and sea were both dark, the estates as private and closed away on this side as on the roadside.

There was no moon, but starshine bounding from the sea outlined everything in shadowed silver. Walls and gates marked the properties, with more of those big urns looming at the corners. Almost all the houses tucked far back in there showed interior lights, but they were far away, screened, indirect; only twice did he see doors open to terrace or lawn, lights and sound spilling seaward, small parties in progress. Both times, he kept his head down so his pale face wouldn't show, and moved closer to the shush of the waves, out of reach of the lights.

He wasn't carrying tonight and was dressed in dark but casual clothing and carried Parmitt's identification. If he were to have a confrontation at all tonight, it would be with cops or private security, and with either one a gun would be more of a problem than a help.

He had tried to count the number of estates down from Melander's, driving here, and now he tried again to count, walking north, but wasn't sure he'd seen them all in either direction. When he came to the one he thought was probably Melander's, it showed toward the sea a seven-foot-high pale concrete wall. In the middle of the wall was a fairly narrow opening, in which a wrought-iron gate stood shut and locked, with concrete steps behind it leading upward, flanked by walls of more concrete.

At the northern edge of the wall, it met the next property's barrier, which was sea grape entwined with chain-link fence, stretching even higher than the neighboring wall. It looked to Parker as though the people who'd built the Melander place, if this was the Melander place, had put up this wall along the beach, and sidewalls back, then filled in behind it to make a high terrace at the same level as the road out front. Instead of that, the people next door had left the slope of the land as it was, down toward the sea, and merely fenced it.

Chain-link fence is a ladder, even when encumbered with sea grape. Seeing only a few lights in the house behind the fence, Parker climbed it at the corner, moving slowly, not wanting to make a lot of noise and also not wanting to leave a trail for Melander and the others to notice tomorrow.

When he was a few feet off the ground, he could see over the top of the wall, and it was lawn at that upper level, stretching back to the house. A few lights glowed inside the house, but there was no sound, no movement. An ornamental wrought-iron fence was fixed along the top of the wall, waist-high, and was most likely there to keep guests from falling off the lawn onto the sand seven feet below.

Parker stepped over the fence onto the ground above and behind the wall, and crouched there, waiting for a response. He knew the kind of security this sort of place could have, but he doubted Melander and Carlson and Ross were keeping it up; they weren't the type. Still, it would be better to be cautious, especially if he'd counted wrong and this wasn't their place after all.

What he waited for now was a motion sensor. That would be the first line of defense for these estates, and it should react to his presence as soon as he was on the property. If this house had such a thing, it would not only sound alarms, it would most likely also switch on floodlights around the exterior of the house, because the residents would be less interested in capturing anybody than in repelling them. If anything happened now, Parker would go over the wrought-iron fence, jump to the sand below, and move south, back toward the car.

But nothing happened. He stood there, waiting, listening, and looked around. The ground where he stood had once been lawn, but hadn't been cared for in a long time; ocean air had killed it, leaving hard crumbly earth. So this was probably the right house.

It loomed ahead of him, pale in the starlight, centered on its property, with broad open swaths that had been lawn on both sides. Screens of tall ficus along both sides blocked any sight of the neighbors, but the ficus wasn't being cared for; instead of the smooth wall-like appearance the professional gardeners would give them, the lines of trees had a messy, shaggy, unshaven look.

After a long minute, Parker moved forward toward the house. It looked as though only two lights were burning in there, one upstairs and one down; almost a guarantee that nobody was home. The lights were dim, amber, deep in the house, but they showed the rectangles of windows and glass doors.

Lawn gave way to stone patio closer to the house. There was no furniture, and sand scraped underfoot. Ahead, a line of glass doors like a theater entrance showed a large dim room. Parker stepped close to the glass to look in.

The light in there came through a broad doorway at the far end. This had once been the main public room of the house, but now there was nothing in it but a piano, pushed at an angle into a far corner, with no bench or stool in front of it.

The doors were locked; naturally. Would the alarm system be functioning, and would it connect with the local police station? Parker didn't think Melander and the others would want police coming around, not for any reason, but there was no need to be hasty or careless.

He stepped back to the outer edge of the patio to look at the second floor. There was a setback up there, and a terrace. And where the house was not glass it was large rectangular blocks of pale stone; not much harder to climb than a chain-link fence.

Parker went to the right rear corner of the building and climbed the stones to the second-floor terrace. Here there were signs of occupancy: three cheap chrome and strap chaises, an upside-down liquor carton used as a table, an empty beer bottle standing on the floor near one of the chaises.

Glass doors led to three rooms up here. The center one had been a library and television room, but was now stripped, the shelves bare. Beyond its interior open door he could see the second-floor light source: a chandelier at the head of a flight of stairs.

The two side doors led to what had been and still were bedrooms, though now very simply furnished with nothing but mattresses. These doors were also locked, but the locks were a joke. Parker opened the one to the bedroom on the right, then stepped back to the outer edge of the terrace to wait for a response.

Nothing. No lights came on, no alarm sounded. Two minutes, three minutes, and no sound of police sirens headed this way. The door he'd opened hung ajar.

Parker crossed the terrace and entered the house. He closed the door behind himself.

It didn't take long to search the place. There were fifteen or sixteen rooms, but Melander and Carlson and Ross were only using five: three bedrooms upstairs, the kitchen and dining room downstairs. They were getting along with a minimal amount of furniture.

And they weren't here. The refrigerator was switched on, but it contained only half a dozen beer bottles, nothing perishable. There was almost no clothing in the bedrooms. There were no towels hanging in any of the bathrooms, though a stack of folded towels was on the floor at the head of the central staircase, as though they'd just come back from a laundry.

So they'd moved in here, they'd established the place, and then they'd gone away. They wouldn't come back until it was time for the heist. Parker could make his own presence here, be waiting for them.

He found two alarm systems, the main one with its control pad by the door from the attached garage, and a supplemental one with a control box in a closet near the front door. Both were switched off. Parker rewired them so that, if they were armed, they would seem to be working but were not.

He went out the front door, leaving it open. He studied the grounds, then went over to look into the Dumpster, which was the largest size, big as a long-haul truck. It was a third full of trash: broken chairs, mirrors, wadded mounds of curtains, things the previous owners had not wanted to take with them. There was no construction debris, though, from the road, this big container would make it look as though construction or reconstruction had to be going on.

Back in the house, he shut the front door and went to the garage, big enough to hold three cars but now standing empty, except for a metal footlocker in a rear corner. The footlocker seemed strange, and was padlocked. Parker crossed to it and studied the padlock, which was new and serious. He lifted one end of the footlocker, and it was very heavy; something metal slid inside there.

So this must be their stash of guns. Parker switched on the garage light long enough to study the footlocker and its padlock, then he switched the light off again, left the garage, left the house, climbed down the neighbors' chain-link fence, and walked back to the Four Seasons. He walked toward the Jaguar, stashed among a dotting of other cars in the dim-lit parking area, then veered off, away from the Jag, moving around into another section of the lot.

There was someone in the Jag. A dark mound, in the passenger seat.

Parker, empty-handed, came slowly at the Jag from the rear, trying to keep out of any mirrors the passenger might see. At the end, he crouched against

the rear bumper and moved his head slowly to the
left until he could see the rearview mirror, see the re-
flection of the person, move farther left, see the person better . . .

Leslie.

4

When he straightened and moved around to her side of the car, she saw him coming and reacted by opening the door. The interior light came on and she squinted, smiling up at him. "Have a nice walk?" she said.

He said, "Who knows you're here?"

"Oh, don't be silly," she said, still smiling, pretending to be unconcerned, but clutching tight to the handle of the open door to hide her nervousness. "I'm no threat to you," she said, "so you don't have any reason to be a threat to me."

He said, "Who knows you're here?"

She was still in uniform, the beige suit and the dolphin pin. She shifted her legs to get out of the car, saying, "Buy me a drink at the bar over there."

He reached out and cupped his palm over the top of her head, feeling the tight blond curls. He didn't exert pressure, just held her there, so she couldn't go on getting out of the car. "Leslie," he said, "when I ask a question, you answer it."

She tried to move her head, to twist out from under his hand, so she could look up at him, but he wouldn't let her move. "You're hurting my neck," she said.

He knew he wasn't, but it didn't matter. "Who knows you're here, Leslie?"

"No one! All right? No one."

He released her and stepped back a pace so she could get out of the car. She did so, tottering a bit as she got to her feet, leaving the door open so she could lean on it and there'd be some light. Sounding resentful and flustered, she said, "You want to know who I told your *business,* is that right?"

That was half of it. The other half was, how complicated would it be if he had to kill her. He said, "What *is* my business, Leslie?"

"That's what I'm trying to figure out," she said.

"You smelled something."

"I certainly did." She was getting her self-confidence back, feeling they would deal in words now and words were her territory. She said, "Everything you did in the car today was almost right, al-most, but I didn't buy it. Is Daniel Parmitt your real name?"

"Why wouldn't it be?"

"Because you're less than two months old," she said. "When we finished driving around today, I thought, That man doesn't really want a house here, but he wants *something,* and the only thing he showed any interest in at all was the house Mr. Roderick bought."

"Roderick."

"Also a Texan, or so he says," she reminded him. "And I looked into him, too, and he's only six months old. The two of you, there isn't a paper, not a line of credit, a history of any kind that goes back even a year."

"I've been out of the country," Parker said.

"You've been off the planet," she told him. "Listen, do we have to stand here in the parking lot? If you won't buy me a drink, I'll buy you one."

He said, "Where do you live?"

"Me?" She seemed surprised at the question. "With my mother and sister," she said, "over in West Palm."

He didn't want a drink with her in a hotel bar, because it was seeming as though she might have to die tonight, and he didn't want to have been seen with her just before. But visiting the mother and the sister in West Palm was also no good, and taking her to his room at the Breakers would be worst of all.

On the other hand, *had* she talked to people about this strange new man? Had she left a note somewhere? He said, "Let's go to your office."

That surprised her. "What for?"

"You have keys, you can get in. We'll have the talk you want to have, and we won't be interrupted."

"I really do want a drink, you know."

"Later."

She frowned at him, trying to work him out.

"Leslie," he said, "where's your car?"

101

"Over there," she said, and pointed generally toward the hotel.

"I'll meet you at your office," he said, and walked around to the driver's side of the Jag.

She hadn't moved. She went on standing there, in the V of the open door, her beige suit bouncing the light, her face in semi-darkness as she frowned at him over the top of the car.

"Shut the door, Leslie," he said. "I'll meet you at your office."

He got into the Jag, and she leaned down to look in at him. "Daniel Parmitt is not your real name," she said, and straightened, and shut the door at last, and walked away across the parking lot.

He left the Jag in the other long block of Worth Avenue, among the very few cars parked there, and walked to the office, where she was waiting for him on the sidewalk. "You could have parked here," she said.

"I like to walk."

She shook her head, turned away, and unlocked the office door. "We'll use Linda's office in the back," she said. "It's more comfortable, and we won't have to leave a lot of lights on in front."

"Fine."

An illuminated clock on the sidewall, gift of an insurance company, served as the office night-light. In its glow, he followed her through the desks to a doorway at the back. She stepped through, hit a switch, and overhead fluorescents came stuttering on.

He said. "Aren't there better lights?"

"Hold on."

The office was wider than deep, with a large desk on the right, filing cabinets across the back, and shelves and cabinets on the left. A dark brown vinyl sofa, with a coffee table, stood out from the cabinets, facing the desk across the way.

While he stood in the doorway, she turned on a brass desk lamp, a tulip-globed floor lamp in the corner behind the desk like something in a funeral parlor, and a group of muted strip lights under the shelves. "You can turn the overheads off right there," she told him, pointing to the switch beside the door.

Now the room was comfortable, illuminated in pools of amber. Crossing to sit on the right side of the sofa, he said, "Tell me what you think you've got so far."

"You're a wooden nickel, that's all I know right now," she said. "Linda usually keeps white wine in the refrigerator here. Want some?"

She herself did, of course: keeping the tension held down below the surface was hard work. He said, "If you do."

She smiled. "At last, a human response."

The refrigerator, a low one, was in a cabinet behind the sofa. Real estate magazines and old newsmagazines were on the black Formica coffee table. She brought a bottle of California chardonnay and two water glasses and shoved magazines out of the way to put them down. The bottle was already open, cork stuck back in, not much gone. She pulled the cork and poured for them both. "To truth," she said, toasting him.

He shrugged, and they both drank, and she sat at the other end of the sofa, knees together, holding the glass in her left hand, body angled toward him. "You're new at your bank," she said, "you're new at your house. One thing you get good at in this business is credit checks, and your credit doesn't exist. You never owned or leased a car before the one you have now, never had a credit card, never had a mortgage, never had a bank account until the one you just started in San Antonio."

"I'm an American citizen," he told her, "but I was born in Ecuador. I don't know if you saw my birth certificate."

"That isn't one of the things I can get at."

"Well, you'll see I was born in Quito of American parents. I've still got family down there, I've lived most of my life down there. The family's in oil."

"Banana oil," she said. "Who is Roderick to you?"

"Nobody."

"That's why you were looking for his house? That's why you walked to his house in the middle of the night?"

"Who says I walked to his house?"

"I do."

He glanced at her shoes, which were medium-heel pumps, not much use on sand. "I just went for a walk," he said.

"Coincidence, you headed straight for Roderick's house."

"Coincidence," he agreed. "You say you've got problems with this Roderick, too."

"Well, I didn't have, until I started thinking about you and looking into who you really are. That led me to run the same thing on Roderick and he's another guy out of a science-fiction movie, suddenly dropped onto the planet from the mother ship five or six months ago."

"Why don't you ask him about himself?"

"I don't know the man, I didn't handle the sale. We carried the house, but it was a different broker made the deal." She sipped wine, put her glass down, leaned toward him. "Let me tell you what I know about Mr. Roderick," she said.

"Go ahead."

"He wanted a presence here on the cheap. There was a house nobody wanted because it should be a teardown, but he wanted it, and now he's got it, and he isn't doing anything with it."

"No?"

"No. There's a general contractor Mr. Roderick was going to hire, to do the renovation work. I called him this afternoon, and Mr. Roderick hasn't got around to starting the work yet. Says he's still dealing with his architect."

"Maybe he is."

"What architect? There's nobody there. The place is empty. Nothing's happening at all."

"Architects are slow sometimes," he said.

"Particularly when they don't exist." She finished the wine in her glass, looked at his, poured herself a second. Before drinking, she said, "Now you show up, and you want to know about Roderick, but you don't want Roderick to know about you."

"You watch too much television," he told her.

"Yes, I do," she said. "And I drink too much. And I worry too much. And I live with my mother and my sister. I'm divorced, and I don't want *that* son of a bitch back, and I don't need any other son of a bitch to take his place, in case you were wondering, but I want more than *this*."

"Uh-huh."

"I want more than driving obnoxious fat cats around to show them empty houses, fending off gropes from ninety-year-olds wearing white ascots— oh, yes, white ascots, and they're all wonderful *dancers*—sitting at my goddam desk out there every day, waiting for my life when my life is *over*."

"Now you're watching too much daytime television," he told her.

"I would if I didn't have to work." Her glass was empty again; she refilled it and said, "I look at you, and I say, what does this man want? He playacts to be somebody that belongs here, but he doesn't belong here. And Roderick doesn't belong here. So who are these people and what do they want?"

"You tell me," Parker said.

"Palm Beach has only got one thing," she told him. "Money."

"Sun and sand," he said. "Parties. Charity balls. Shopping on Worth Avenue."

She laughed. "I'd like to see you shopping on

Worth Avenue," she said. "I really would. You could buy a white ascot."

"I might."

"Daniel—I'm going to call you Daniel, because I have to call you something, so, Daniel, what *I* need, to get out of here, to get a running jump on a new life, is *money*. And what you are here for, and what Roderick is here for, is money."

"You want me to give you some money," he suggested.

"Oh, Daniel," she said, and shook her head. "Dan? No, Daniel. Daniel, I don't want you to *give* me money. Do you really think I'm stupid? Do you really think I don't know why you parked a block away and didn't want to be seen with me in a public place?"

"Why's that, Leslie?"

"Because if I'm a problem," she said, and sat up straight, and looked evenly at him, "you intend to kill me."

"Leslie," he said, "while you're watching all this television, I think you've also been smoking some weed."

She brushed that aside. "I'm being serious," she said. "I want to *earn* the money. Do I go to you, or do I go to Roderick? I've met you—"

"And Roderick isn't here," he pointed out. "At least you tell me he isn't here."

"So here's what I'm telling you now," she said. "Whatever you have in mind, robbery, I suppose, or maybe a kidnapping, kidnap one of these dowagers here, whatever it is, you need somebody who knows the territory."

"You."

"Why not me? I sell real estate, I've been in probably a third of the important houses around here, and I know the rest. I know the town, I can answer questions, and I can tell you what questions you're forgetting to ask. Roderick doesn't have anybody local, and I think you and Roderick are competitors, so if you have me you have an advantage over him."

He watched her, thinking about what she was saying, who she was, what she wanted.

She gave him another level look; she didn't show any nervousness at all now. "To even find Roderick," she reminded him, "you had to come play that roundabout game with me. And all it did was make me suspicious. How many people do you want wondering about you?"

"None," he said.

"It's too late for none, but I can help you limit it to one."

He picked up his glass and sipped from it. She watched him, and then said, "One thing. I'm not talking about sex."

He looked at her. "I didn't think you were."

She said, "I find it a strain just to talk with you. I certainly don't ever want to take my clothes off in front of you."

"But you're going to have to," he said.

She shook her head. "No, I—"

"I mean, you're going to have to now," he said.

She stared at him, panic leaching through. "I can't—I thought you—"

"Leslie," he said, "I have to know if you're wearing a wire."

She gaped, trying to make sense of the words. "What?"

"A wire. I have to know. One way or another, Leslie, I have to know."

"You mean—" She was blinking a lot, catching up with the situation. "You mean you think I could be taping you?"

"Come on, Leslie."

"But—I wouldn't, I don't—honestly, no."

"Now, Leslie. You stand up over there, and I'll sit here, and you'll show me whether or not you're wearing a wire."

"I'm not," she said, her voice fainter.

"Good. Show."

"And then what?"

"If you're not wired, I leave here and walk back to my car, while you turn the lights off and lock the place. Tomorrow, you bring Linda another bottle of wine, and I'll be in touch. Now, Leslie."

She wasn't wearing a wire.

5

Her last name was Mackenzie. The phone book gave her a listing on Utica Street in West Palm Beach. The reverse phone book also gave a listing for Laurel Simons at the same address.

Parker left the phone company building and drove the Jag across Flagler Bridge out of Palm Beach and through West Palm to the airport, where he left it in long-term parking and walked around the lot until he found a red Subaru Outback station wagon, a much less noticeable car than a yellow Jaguar convertible, in any neighborhood except Palm Beach. It had almost no dust on it, so it hadn't been here long. Breaking into it, he hot-wired the ignition and drove to the exit, where he turned in the ticket he'd just picked up.

The tollbooth clerk, a Hispanic who looked or

tried to look like Pancho Villa, frowned at the ticket: "You don't stay long."

"I forgot my passport," Parker told him. "I've gotta go back and get it, screwed up my whole day."

"Tough," the clerk said, gave Parker his change, and Parker drove to Utica Street.

It was a neat but inexpensive neighborhood of single-family homes on small plots, most with an attached garage. Basketball hoops over the garage doors, neatly maintained lawns, tricycles and toys around some front doors. A lot of aluminum siding in shades of off-white or pastels.

Number 417 was ranch-style, two stories on the left with the garage below and most likely bedrooms above, one story on the right. The garage door was closed, with a green Honda Accord parked at the edge of the blacktop driveway, out of the way of access to the garage. So Leslie's Lexus, being more important to their livelihood, got the garage, and the mother's car got the weather.

Parker circled the block once, then stopped in front of a house half a block short of 417. There was a Florida map in the driver's door pouch; he opened it on the steering wheel.

This was a working-class neighborhood, and everybody was away working. Very few cars drove down Utica Street, and no pedestrians appeared at all. It was now eleven-thirty in the morning; Parker was ready to wait until schoolchildren started to return this afternoon.

But he didn't have to. At twenty to one, the front

door at 417 opened and two women came out. One was an older, bulkier version of Leslie, with a harsher blond in her short hair and an angry thrust to her head and a similar conservative taste in clothing. The other was gross; she wore a many-colored muumuu and she waddled. Her black hair was fixed in a bad home permanent, a thousand tight ringlets like fiddlehead ferns, as though in a lunatic attempt to distract from the body. She tripped on the driveway, over nothing at all, and her mother snapped at her. The daughter cringed and lumbered on.

The two women got into the car, the mother at the wheel, and drove away. After lunch, they go out and shop for dinner. Parker drove the Subaru closer, stopping in front of the house next door, then got out of the car, walked around to the back of the house, and forced the kitchen door.

There wasn't much he needed to know—Leslie was hardly a mystery woman—and he found it all in fifteen minutes. Her former husband was named Gerald Mackenzie, he lived in Miami, and there was cold, correct, formal communication between them if something like old taxes caused them to make contact with one another.

Leslie kept small debts going in several credit card and department store accounts. She didn't seem to have a man in her life, and maybe hadn't since the no-fault divorce from Gerald eight years earlier. She had occasional correspondence with a woman friend in New Jersey.

She had not written anything anywhere about her

discoveries concerning Daniel Parmitt. She didn't seem to own a gun, unless it was in the glove compartment of the Lexus.

She was the alpha member of the family. Her room, facing the backyard from above the garage, was larger than the other two bedrooms up here, and had its own bath. She'd made an office out of a corner of the room, with a small desk and a low filing cabinet and a computer hooked to the Internet. She had done her best to make herself comfortable and at home here, and her mother and sister had done what they could to help, but it hadn't worked. Her room was impersonal, and she was willing to take a leap into the unknown rather than stay in this life.

What she had said last night, about him needing somebody local to smooth the way, made sense. The question was, did *she* make sense? The move she'd made was a strange one; did it mean more strange moves ahead?

Most people in Leslie's position wouldn't have been bothered by his Daniel Parmitt imitation, wouldn't have noticed anything wrong with it. Of the few people who might have picked up his errors, or seen a glimpse of his actual self under his performance, what were the likely reactions? First, most common, to do nothing, to chalk it up to eccentricity. Second, if really snagged by some false note somewhere, to mention it to a friend, somebody in the office, or a member of the family at home, and maybe even follow up with a conversation with a local cop; more likely if the person already knew a local

113

cop. But the least probable reaction, Parker thought, was what Leslie had done: follow the ringer, try to figure him out, try to use him for her own purposes, which was to get out of this dead-end life and start over somewhere else.

So she was quick, and she didn't let her fear hold her back. And she didn't intend to get cute and try to use sex as a weapon, as she'd demonstrated last night by her awkwardness and discomfort when she'd had to very briefly strip.

So did all that mean she was reliable, or did it mean she was a loose cannon? There was nothing in her house to tell him for sure. For the moment, then, make use of her, but keep watch.

Before he left the house, he phoned her at the real estate office. "Leslie, it's Daniel Parmitt."

"Oh, Mr. Parmitt," she said. "I was wondering if I'd hear from you again."

"Today," he said, "I'm interested in looking at some condos."

"Very different."

"Very. Around four o'clock? You have a nice one to show me?"

"Does it need to be furnished?"

"Doesn't matter."

"Good," she said, sounding relieved. "There's a lovely two-bedroom in the Bromwich, ocean view. I could meet you in the lobby."

"Fine," he said, and hung up, and drove the Subaru back to the airport. He left it in its old spot in long-term parking, picked up the Jaguar, and drove to the exit.

This clerk was a Hispanic woman, chunky and bored, who said, "You come in today? This the long-term."

"I forgot my passport, gotta go back for it, screws up the whole day."

"Tough," she said, and gave him his change.

6

The condos along the narrow strip of island south of the main part of Palm Beach yearn toward a better life: something English, somewhere among the landed gentry. The craving is there in the names of the buildings: the Windsor, the Sheffield, the Cambridge. But whatever they call themselves, they're still a line of pale concrete honeycombs on a sandbar in the sun.

Parker arrived at the Bromwich at five after four. Two Hispanic gardeners worked on the long bed of fuchsia and impatiens along the low ornamental wall in front with the place's name on it in block gold letters. Signs at the entrance indicated residents' parking to the right, visitors' to the left. The visitors' area was farther from the building.

Parker drove to the gleaming blacktop expanse of the visitors' parking lot and left the Jag next to Leslie's blue Lexus. He walked through the sun to the boxy cream-colored building, seeing none of the residents, though the other lot was full of their cars, mostly big old-fashioned boats, traditional Detroit iron.

The lobby was amber faux marble with a uniformed black security guard at a long chest-high kidney-shaped faux-marble desk. The lobby seating was several round puffs of magenta sofa; Leslie rose from one of them. Today her suit was peach, her pin a gold rose. "Mr. Parmitt," she said with her working-hours smile, and came forward to shake his hand. "Right on time."

"Afternoon, Ms. Mackenzie," he said. Her hand was soft and dry and without pressure.

She turned to the guard to say, "We're looking at 11-C, Jimmy."

"Yes, ma'am." He gave Parker a disinterested look, then looked downward again. He had the *Globe* newspaper open on his desk, among the phone systems and security screens.

The elevators were around behind the desk. As they rode up together, she said, "You don't want a condo, you want a place to talk."

He shrugged. "What else?"

"So I'm hired," she said with a bland smile, as though it hardly mattered.

He said, "It doesn't work exactly that way."

"You'll explain it," she said, and the elevator slowed to a stop.

He waited for her to lead the way, but instead of leaving the elevator she held down the button that would keep the door open and said, "If you have to check me for a wire again today, we'll leave now."

He shook his head. "Once was enough."

"It certainly was," she said, and led the way out of the elevator and down to unlock them into 11-C.

It was completely empty, as bright and bare as the beach down below. Their shoes made echoing sounds on the blond wood floor, bouncing off the hard white walls and, in the living room, the uncurtained wall of glass doors that opened to the balcony. The place had been repainted, to make it ready for sale, and the smell of the paint was a faint tang in the air.

Parker crossed to open the sliding balcony door. It was hot out here, but with a breeze. The afternoon shadow of the building lay on the beach down below, where no one sat or swam.

Pink plastic-sheet walls on both sides shielded the view of the balconies to right and left, and openwork iron benches were built into both of those walls. Pointing to one of them, "We'll sit here," he said.

"You have to know," she told him, "that wall isn't soundproof."

The outer edge of the balcony was a waist-high pink plastic-sheet wall, with a black iron railing along the top. Parker held to it, leaned forward, and looked around the outer edge of the privacy wall at the balcony next door. Potted plants filled the bench he could see over there, and the rest of the space was occupied by a white plastic table, four chairs to match, a gas grill, and a StairMaster. That apartment's glass wall was completely shielded inside with white drapes. There was no one on the balcony.

He leaned back to turn and say, "There's nobody there."

She was wide-eyed, both hands pressed to her chest. "Don't do that," she said.

"Sit down, Leslie."

They sat side by side on the iron bench against the pink wall, he facing inward, she facing the view. He said, "I'm going to tell you what's going on."

"All right," she said. Now she looked solemn, as though she were being inducted into somebody's secret rites, like the Masons or Cosa Nostra.

He said, "Don't ask me any questions, because I'm only going to tell you what I want to tell you."

"I understand."

"All right. The guy you know as Roderick owes me some money."

She looked disappointed. "It's some kind of debt?"

"Some kind. He's with two other guys. Have you seen them?"

"I've never even seen Roderick."

"Well, the three came here with just enough cash to put the down payment on that house. Some of the cash they used was mine."

She said, "Do they intend to roll it over? Don't tell me they have a buyer."

"Leslie, listen," he said. "What they are is thieves. I don't mean from me, I mean that's what they do, who they are."

"You, too," she said.

He said, "They want the house because there's a

job going down and they know they can't get off the island afterwards."

"If anything big happens," she said, "they raise all the drawbridges. And they patrol the Waterway very seriously."

"That's why they don't want to have to leave. They want to be established here, already known and not suspect. If I rented this condo here right now, and two weeks from now it happens, the cops would be at the door, they'd want to know all about me."

"And you two months old," she said.

"So that's why Melander—he's Roderick—that's why he wanted to be already in place, nobody wondering about him."

"They're going to do a big robbery," she said, "and then go back to that house and wait for the excitement to die down."

"That's right."

"But they used your money to buy the house."

"A quarter of it."

"For the down payment," she said. "So when they do this robbery, you're going to be there to get your part of the money back."

"To get it all, Leslie," he said. "They shouldn't have taken my money."

She studied him. "You mean that."

"Of course I mean it."

She nodded, thinking about this. "So it's a lot of money."

"Yes."

"And some of it will come to me, because I'm not cheating you, I'm helping you."

"Yes."

"If they hadn't cheated you, you would take a quarter."

"Yes."

She looked past him, out at the ocean. "This is a little scarier than I thought," she said. He waited, and she looked at him again. She said, "You're here to find out if you can trust me, and I'm here to find out if I can trust you, and if either of us guesses wrong, we're in trouble."

"That's right."

"But I think," she said, "if I guess wrong, I can be in a lot worse trouble than you."

"Trouble is trouble," he said.

"Maybe so. What is this robbery?"

"That's the first thing you can do for me," he said. "You can tell me what the robbery is."

"You don't know?"

"I know some things about it. I know it's a charity thing."

"There are charity events all season," she told him. "There are balls here that are five thousand dollars a ticket. But that isn't cash."

"Neither is this," he said. "It's a charity auction of jewelry. It's sometime probably in the next two weeks, and they told me the market value of the jewelry was twelve million dollars. Can you tell me what it is?"

She looked surprised, and then she laughed. As though disbelieving, she said, "Mrs. Clendon's jewels?"

121

"Is that it?"

"That's it, oh, absolutely, that's it." She seemed to find the whole thing very funny. "Oh, Daniel," she said, "and I had such hopes."

"What do you mean?"

"There's nothing there to help anybody, Daniel," she said. "There's nothing for me, and there's nothing for you, and there's nothing for your friend Roderick."

"They're gonna do it."

"Then they're going to jail," she said. "And if you're there, you'll go to jail." She rose, stood facing him. "But I won't be there," she said. "Don't worry, Daniel, I'm going to forget this entire conversation." She turned away, toward the living room.

He said, "Leslie." When she looked back at him, he said, "Unless you want to go off the balcony, Leslie, you'll sit down."

She gave a frightened look at the air beyond the balcony railing. "They'd know you're in the building," she said.

"Let me worry about that."

They looked at each other. He was deciding to stand when she came over and sat beside him. "If I tell you about it," she said, "and if you see it can't work, will you let me go?"

"Yes," he said.

"Daniel," she said, "I really wish it was something that could work. I could taste it, Daniel."

"Freedom."

"The new me."

Parker said, "Tell me about Mrs. Clendon, Leslie."

7

The first thing you ought to know, Leslie told him, is that there are no basements in Palm Beach, the water table is too high. And the rich people are seasonal, they're *never* here between May and November, so they need somewhere to store all their valuables while they're gone, and for the last fifty years that place has been the First National Bank.

The First National Bank doesn't just have safe-deposit boxes like other banks, they have entire vaults down under the bank. They store about three thousand fur coats down there every summer, and everything else people don't want to leave in their empty houses: rare wines, gun collections, paintings, silverware and goldware, even furniture, antique chairs and things like that.

You don't want to break in there, believe me you don't; the bank is very serious about its responsibilities. The closest anybody ever came to robbing that bank was back in 1979, when a college student got into a crate and had himself shipped into the bank as antiques. His idea was to come out of the crate at night, fill it up with valuable things, and then wait to slip out of the bank during regular business hours. Then he'd come back later to get the crate. Except the bank is guarded at night, and he was found before he could get out.

Even now, during the season, the bank is full of valuables. The rich women keep all their most expensive jewelry in the bank, and the bank opens up late every night that there's one of the important charity balls. They open so the women can come get their stuff, and then they open again later that night so they can bring it all back. Somebody told me the mirror down there by the vaults isn't regular glass; it's tinted gray because that makes people look better when they're trying on their jewels. So the bank takes very good care of its customers.

One of the most important customers the bank ever had was Miriam Hope Clendon. On the Hope side, her family was important in transatlantic shipping up till the Second World War, when they sold everything and became the idle rich. The same thing on the Clendon side, except they were railroads out west.

By the time you got to Miriam Hope Clendon, the money was so old it didn't have any bad suggestions of trade on it anymore; it was as though Miriam Hope Clendon had money only because God wanted her to. So naturally she was very important in Palm Beach, and important to the bank. And also she lived longer than anybody—she was something like ninety-seven when she finally died, in Maine, last August.

Her family didn't live as long as she did, and most of her children didn't have children, or if they did the children died in accidents or suicide, so when she passed away she was the last of her line except for some very distant cousins, none of whom had ever even met her or had ever been to Palm Beach. Still, they'll get most of what she left.

But not all of it. One of the assistant managers in the bank had become a kind of pal of hers in her last years, when she didn't have anybody else except employees, and he was very interested in raising money for the library here. It's only the last few years there even *is* a library in Palm Beach. He talked to Miriam about the library sometimes, and she contributed some money every once in a while, but it wasn't much of a big deal.

But then she died, and in her will she left all the jewelry she'd kept in the bank to this manager, not for himself, but to do a charity auction and raise money for the library. They'd known each other in the first place because of her jewels, so that's what made her think about doing it that way.

The auction and the ball—there has to be a ball, of course—were set up by a couple of the women who do all that sort of thing here, with the man from the bank to consult. *Everybody* wants some of the Miriam Hope Clendon jewelry, because she used to knock

125

their socks off at the charity balls, glittering like a chandelier. And the ball is going to be a week from this Thursday, with the auction the next night.

So right now, all that jewelry is still in the vault in the bank, and you aren't going to get at it in there, and neither is Roderick, or whatever his name is. On the Wednesday before the ball, the jewelry is *all* going to be transported by armored car to the Breakers, because the Breakers has the biggest ballroom on the island, and that's where it's going to be displayed, under *heavy* guard, during the ball on Thursday, so people can see it all, under glass and behind electrified fencing.

Then on Friday, the display will be taken down and it will all be moved over to the Fritz estate, because now Mrs. Helena Stockworth Fritz is the most important person in Palm Beach society, now that Miriam Hope Clendon is dead, and Mrs. Fritz insisted the auction be held at her house. *Hundreds* of people are invited to the ball on Thursday, but to go to the auction on Friday you have to make a contribution to the library fund and you have to make a sealed bid on at least one piece in the collection. So no freeloaders.

I'm not sure exactly when the jewelry's all going back to the bank, either late Friday night or early Saturday morning, but that's what's going to happen. The successful bidders won't get to take the jewelry home with them from the auction; they'll have to go to the bank the next Monday morning and show their bidding slip and collect their jewelry then.

So what's going to happen is, this huge collection of very important and very valuable jewelry is going to leave the bank on Wednesday, under extremely heavy guard. It's going to the Breakers to be set up along the sides of the ballroom. Then after the dance it's going to be moved to Mrs. Fritz's house, still with the same armored car and guards, and it'll be guarded all the time it's there, and after the auction it's going back, all together, to the bank. I don't know what your friends have in mind, but if they're going to try to break into the bank, they'll be caught. If they try to steal it all from the Breakers or from Mrs. Fritz's house, they'll never get out. If they try to attack the armored car on any one of its three trips, they'll probably be shot. The people here know what Mrs. Clendon's jewels are worth—they're not going to just leave them lying around.

I'm sorry to have to tell you this, Leslie finished, because I'd like them to get their money, so you can get your money, so I can get my money. But it isn't going to happen. Forget it.

8

The shadow of the building was a little longer, reaching out across the sand toward the sea. Out near the horizon two boats, widely separated, both slid south. Parker stood and paced, and she watched him. After a minute, he stopped and put his hand on the railing and looked out at the sea. He said, "This Mrs. Fritz's house. I'm thinking it's on the ocean but it doesn't have a beach."

"No, it doesn't," she said, sounding a little surprised. "It's a seawall along there. It's not far from where that drifting cargo ship ran onto somebody's terrace a few years ago."

"I know these guys," Parker said. "They're gaudy. They're going to like Mrs. Fritz's house because it isn't a commercial space, it's a private space, so control can never be one hundred percent. They're going to like it because they can come in from the sea, go back out to the sea, and duck right back in again down at their own place, while everybody's searching the Atlantic Ocean for them."

"It isn't that easy," she insisted.

"They don't expect it to be easy," he told her. "They expect it to be tough, and that's why they'll be gaudy. I don't know what they have in mind, but it'll shake people up."

"If you mean scare them," Leslie said, "it would take a lot to scare people in Palm Beach. Not so long ago, you had a militia of these octogenarians on the beach, still in their white pants, with their big-game hunting rifles, marching back and forth on the sand, drilling, ready to repel Castro."

"Good thing for them Castro didn't show up," Parker said. "But the point is, Leslie, I'm not going to steal the package, Melander and the others are. I don't have to have a plan, I just have to know what theirs is. But I know them, I know what business they're in, I know they're sure enough of themselves to sink all their cash into this thing, and I know how their minds work. They won't mess with bank vaults, and they won't try to get into the middle of a huge hotel on its own acres of grounds. An armored car on this island is hopeless—where would you take it? So that leaves Mrs. Fritz, in a private house on the ocean with a seawall. That's where they're going to do it, so the question is when."

"After everybody's gone home," she suggested, "and before the jewels are loaded back into the armored car."

"No. I told you, these guys are gaudy, they won't want to sneak in and out. A lot of rich people all dressed up in one confined place, wearing their *own* big-dollar jewels. That's the time to come in, when you can make the maximum trouble, the maximum panic. What are guards gonna do if there's a thousand important people running back and forth screaming?"

"I don't know," she said.

"They won't do a lot of shooting," he said.

"No, I suppose not."

He said, "Show me Mrs. Fritz's house."

"I can't take you *in* there," she said, surprised. "It isn't on the market."

"Drive me by it."

"You won't see much, but all right. We'll take my car. We'd better find a place where you can put yours in some shade."

"Good."

She stood and looked out at the ocean. "Are they really going to do that, do you think? Come in from the sea?"

"That's their style."

"Like James Bond," she said.

He shook his head. "More like *Jaws*," he told her.

9

Mrs. Fritz's mansion was invisible from anywhere, except, probably, the ocean. Parker and Leslie drove past it twice, first northbound and then southward again, and both times she drove as slowly as she could when they went by, but there was nothing to be seen.

An eight-foot-high stucco-covered wall in a kind of beige color, dappled with climbing ivies, faced the road and ran back both sides of the property. In the dead middle of the road-facing wall a broad opening was filled by massive wood-beam doors, vertical planks held together with thick black bands of iron. These must be electrically operated, and would only be opened when Mrs. Fritz or some other acceptable person was going in or out.

"You see what I mean," Leslie said, the second time they drove by it.

"Those doors will be open the night of the auction," Parker said.

"With security standing there and a Palm Beach police car in the driveway. You don't crash Mrs. Fritz's parties."

"Melander will."

She dropped him back at the Jaguar, in the corner of a real estate office parking lot where tall sea grape offered some shade. "What now?" she said.

"We wait for party time," he said, and got out of the car.

To get where he was going next, he had to drive past Mrs. Fritz's estate one more time, and the thing was just impossible. There was no parking along here, no useful shoulder, nowhere even to stop. You couldn't find anywhere to sit and watch the place.

Well, that wasn't Parker's problem. That was somebody else's problem.

He drove over to West Palm, parked the Jag a little after five-thirty, and found a hardware store open, where he bought a cordless drill and an inch-wide metal-routing bit and a small hacksaw and a glass cutter and a pair of pliers and a roll of clear tape and two rubber suction cups with handles. Then he drove back to the Breakers and, in one of the shops off the lobby, bought a bright blue canvas shoulder bag with a flap. Everything from the hardware store went into it.

That night, with the shoulder bag, he left the Jag in the Four Seasons parking lot and walked to Melander's house. This time he was armed, carrying the

Sentinel in his hand so he could toss it into the sea if he had to.

But he didn't have to, so when he got to the house he put the Sentinel in the shoulder bag with the rest of the tools. He went in through the same second-floor bedroom as the last time and then down to the kitchen, where the refrigerator was exactly as it had been before, nothing added or subtracted. So they hadn't yet come back.

He switched lights on as he moved through the house to the garage, where he tipped the footlocker onto its face and drilled an inch-wide round hole through the metal as close as possible to the bottom right corner.

The rear of the footlocker was stiffened with bands of metal that divided it into six sections. Parker hacksawed three sides of the lower right section, then peeled it open and looked inside at the six guns lying in a jumbled heap: three shotguns and three Colt .45 automatics.

One by one he snaked the guns out of the footlocker, then carried them all away to the kitchen. He put them on the table there, sat in front of them, and misaligned the firing pins on the automatics and drained the shot from the shotgun shells. Then he carried them all back to the garage and dropped them into the footlocker. He bent the opened flap down flush again and used the clear tape to put the round plug he'd cut out back into position. If anybody were to open the footlocker and study the interior, the cut would be obvious, but the three wouldn't be looking at the footlocker, they'd be looking at the guns.

Back in the house, he went to the dining room, the only other downstairs room beside the kitchen that they'd furnished, with a simple black Formica Parsons table and three mismatched armless kitchen chairs, all probably bought used over in West Palm. Two floor lamps in the corners gave light, the original chandelier having been messily removed.

If he were in here with them, it would be because they were in control and they wanted a conversation. Would they sit and have him stand? No, they'd rather be the ones on their feet. On which side of the table?

There were three doorways in three walls in here, two broad ones opposite each other opening onto living rooms at the front and rear, and a narrower one with a swing door leading to the kitchen. They would want him with his back to the fourth wall because, without thinking about it, they wouldn't want to be looking at escape routes behind him.

The good thing about a Parsons table is that it has a strip of wood all around, just under the top, that creates a recess. Parker taped the Sentinel to the underside of the tabletop, on the side where there was no door. Then he went looking for a window.

The exterior doors, upstairs and down, were all large expanses of plate glass, too big to be of use. But on the road side of the house, flanking the front door, were pairs of double-hung windows with panes, four over four. Going outside, he chose the corner window farthest from the door and the garage. First he fixed the suction cups onto the top right pane of the lower half of the window, then used the glass cutter to slice the glass through just inside the wooden sash bars, scoring it four times all the way around before he got completely through. Tugging on the suction cups, he removed the rectangle of glass, then made sure he could reach the lock inside. Then he put the pane back in place, fixing it there with small pieces of the clear tape. The suction cups he buried under the shrubbery along the footing.

Walking back along the beach toward the Four Seasons, one by one he threw into the sea the drill, the routing bit, the hacksaw, the glass cutter, the pliers, and the roll of tape. The shoulder bag he left on the ground in the parking lot; some tourist would take it home.

10

The question was Leslie. She'd been useful, but she was an amateur, and an amateur is never entirely reliable. Could she be useful again? Or could she be a problem?

So far, she was doing everything right. She came up with the answers he needed, and she didn't ask a lot of her own unnecessary questions. She didn't try to push herself closer to the job. She showed patience. All of these were rare qualities in an amateur and were keeping her alive.

So the real question was, how tight a leash should he keep on her until the day? He finally decided the answer was to keep no leash at all. If she kept herself to herself, as she'd been doing, fine. If she started phoning, or coming around, he'd deal with it.

It was ten days till the job. There was nothing to do now but wait, and make sure that when Melander and the others came back they didn't notice Parker in the neighborhood. So why not go back to Miami for a few days, spend some time with Claire?

He left in late morning, took Interstate 95 south, and got off the highway at Fort Lauderdale to find a diner lunch. After, he came out of the diner to the bright sunlit parking lot, and the Jaguar was gone.

Stupid; to let that get ripped off. He looked around the parking lot for another car to take, and a guy came out of the diner behind him, working at his mouth with a toothpick. He said, "Hot day."

"Yes," Parker said. He waited for the guy to go away.

But the guy pointed across the parking lot with his toothpick and said, "You see that white Toyota Land Cruiser over there?"

Parker didn't look at the white Toyota Land Cruiser, he looked at the guy with the toothpick. He was bulked up, tanned, about forty, grinning like a man with a secret. He nodded, not looking at Parker, and said, "There's a guy in there with a thirty ought six—you do *anything* he doesn't like, any single thing at all, he'll blow your head off."

"Maybe he'll hit you," Parker said.

"Funny thing about Herby," the guy said. "He never misses what he aims at. Never been known to happen. Why don't we go over there, he can tell you about it himself."

Now Parker looked at the Land Cruiser, a Land Rover clone, then back at the guy. These people weren't from Melander and Carlson and Ross; that trio would handle their own problems. He didn't see how they could be connected with Leslie. So who were they and what was their interest?

The guy said, "I'm walking over there now myself. If you don't walk with me, they'll be hosing down the pavement here later."

Parker said, "We'll walk together. I'm trying to remember where I know you from."

The guy chuckled, not as though he thought Parker had said something funny, but as though it was a skill he'd learned one time, chuckling, and he liked to practice from time to time. As they walked across the parking lot to the Land Cruiser, that was the only answer he gave.

Herby, a sharp-nosed skinny man in a wrinkled white dress shirt and black pants and mirror-lensed aviator sunglasses, sat in the back seat, the big hunting rifle on his lap, right hand loose near the trigger, left hand loose under the barrel. There was no way to tell if he was looking at Parker or not, but it really didn't make any difference.

The first guy, still cheerful, said, "You can ride up front with me."

They were willing to kill him in public, if they had to, but they'd rather do it in private. So there was still a little time. Parker went around to the right side of the Land Cruiser and opened the door, and saw a small square photo on the passenger seat. He picked it up, slid onto the seat, shut the door, and looked at the photo. It was himself, one of the pictures Bobby had taken for his driver's license.

He looked from the picture to the guy, now behind the wheel, grinning at him around the toothpick. "So Norte's dead," Parker said, and dropped the photo out the window.

The guy stuck the key in the ignition. "Hell, pal," he said as the engine started, "everybody's dead. Some people just don't know it yet."

11

They were going to kill him in the Everglades. A good place for it, obviously; the idea had been thought of before.

The white Land Cruiser headed out westward along Alligator Alley, the Everglades Parkway, a two-lane black binding tape laid on the uncertain green land, straight as a rifle shot across the flat landscape. Big trucks groaned along, and the smaller cars zipped around them and sped on. The guy with the toothpick in the rear corner of his mouth moved the Land Cruiser along at a steady unhurried speed. There was time enough to get the job done.

Parker thought about the Sentinel, now taped to the underside of the Parsons table in Melander's dining room. There were two guns stashed in the Jaguar, but he had nothing on his body. Here there was Herby in the back seat with his rifle and maybe some

140

other things. The driver wasn't obviously armed, but he could have a pistol in a pants pocket or in a spring-loaded holster under the dash on the far side of the steering column.

They couldn't do anything on this road, with this traffic. There were always at least half a dozen vehicles in sight. They'd have to turn off, and that was the point where he'd have to make his move. They were pros, and they would know that was when he'd have to move, but he had to anyway. And they knew that, too.

Although it didn't matter now, he couldn't help but wonder if it would have made a difference if he'd decided not to let Julius Norte live. He'd thought the man could handle himself against the fellow who'd sent those killers after him, but maybe without Bobby, Norte hadn't been so invulnerable anymore.

It seemed to Parker that this guy, whoever he was, who'd hired these two in the Land Cruiser, would have been on Daniel Parmitt's trail whether he'd left Norte dead or alive. There would have been papers in Norte's office, evidence, things Parker wouldn't have had the time or knowledge to find and destroy, to tell who the other customer had been that day, who'd dealt himself a hand. It was revenge that guy wanted now, as well as his grim determination to leave nobody alive who could possibly lead back to him. Nothing to do with Parker, but he was stuck in it anyway.

They drove for over an hour, passing the occasional tourist place, offering cold drinks or airboat rides into the swamp or views of caged alligators, and no one in the car spoke. The air-conditioning kept everything cool and dry. They passed small side roads from time to time, bumping away on rough bridges over the canals, and Parker waited.

Over an hour. The driver lowered his visor because the afternoon sun was rolling down the sky, dead ahead, and Parker did the same. There were warnings on notices attached to this side of the visor, but he didn't read them.

The driver tapped the brake. Parker squinted, and maybe that was a road out there, still some distance off, leading to the right. He became very still, and the driver tapped the brake again, and the rifle barrel came to rest against the base of Parker's skull, just below and behind his left ear, a cold hard smoothness of metal.

Parker sensed, but didn't turn his head to see, the driver grin. Still facing front, feeling the steel against his skull, he said, "Try not to jounce on the turn."

The driver practiced his chuckle again, and slowed some more, flipping on his directional.

It was a dirt road, heading north over the scrub near the highway, then going on into the ripe green of the swamp shrubbery. Parker watched it coming and knew he couldn't do the move, not now. He'd have to wait until they thought he wasn't going to do anything. Eventually, they'd believe he'd given up the idea of doing anything, because eventually everybody gives up, and they'd know that. Eventually, he, too, might give up.

The driver made the turn, smooth and slow, but then they bumped a little when they crossed the wooden bridge over the nearby canal, and the rifle barrel jounced hard against his skull, but the gun didn't go off. And a minute later, with the car up to a good speed again and the mangroves and palmettos getting closer, the rifle barrel went away.

Parker adjusted the air-conditioner vent so it wouldn't blow directly on him. He looked at the driver, who concentrated now more completely on his driving on this imperfect road, then twisted around to look back at Herby, who was seated sideways in the left corner back there, so he could hold the rifle with its trigger handy to his right hand and its barrel aimed at the back of Parker's seat. The aviator glasses reflected Parker, darkly. He faced front again.

Once in the swamp, the road veered left and right to keep on the dry ground. Water glinted among the trunks on both sides. The road was one lane wide, but here and there were wider spots where one car could pass another.

A straight stretch, and down at the end a sharp curve to the left. The driver accelerated, and Parker watched his foot on the pedal. At the end of this stretch, he'd have to brake.

There. The foot started to lift, and Parker moved everything at once. His left foot mashed down on the driver's foot and the accelerator, jolting them forward, maybe spoiling Herby's aim for just a second. His right hand shoved the door open against that acceleration as his left hand swung up backhanded to mash that toothpick into the driver's mouth. And his right foot shoved down and leftward, propelling him backward out of the Land Cruiser, as the crack of the rifle shot banged around inside the car.

He landed hard on his back, the Land Cruiser spraying dirt back at him as the driver tried to brake, to steer, to keep the Land Cruiser from running off into the swamp. Herby was rolling out of the car on the other side, not waiting for it to stop, rolling with the rifle cupped against his chest under his crossed arms.

Parker rolled away from the road, hoping for water, but a low berm had been built along here to keep the swamp away from the road, and it stopped him. He had to rise, not wanting to, if he would get over the berm, and as he came up on his knees he heard the crack behind him, much smaller in the outer air, just a firecracker. Except that a punch in the back threw him forward across the top of the berm, and when he lifted himself, suddenly very heavy, there was blood spreading across the front of his shirt. The bullet had gone through him.

He *shoved* with his arms, but they were heavy as trees and he only dropped forward, rolling onto his back. There was no sky, only the darkness of the leaves.

He felt their feet when they rolled him down into the water, but when he hit the water he wasn't feeling anything anymore.

THREE

1

He wasn't there. The house at Colliver Pond was empty, and that was bad news. Melander and Carlson and Ross wandered the empty rooms, looked out the windows at the frozen lake, and they were not happy.

Dissension had started among them not twenty minutes after they'd left Parker at the motel in Evansville, with a handful of earnest money instead of his share of the bank job. Carlson had started it; being the driver, he was the brooder, the one with extra thinking time on his hands. "I don't like it," he'd said.

The other two had known immediately what he was talking about, and Melander had said, "Hal, we didn't have a choice. We thought he'd come in. Tom Hurley would've come in."

"But Hurley left. And he sent us this guy Parker, and I can't help thinking we made a mistake."

"No choice," Melander said again.

"We had choices," Carlson told him, keeping his eye on the road, Interstate 64, headed east, going to switch to 75 southbound at Lexington, aimed for Palm Beach.

Ross, seated beside Carlson up front, with Melander in back, said, "What choices, Hal? The Clendon jewels is the only thing we got, and this is the only way to get it."

"If we were going to rob him—"

"Hey!" Surprised, a little angry, Melander said, "Rob him! Who, Parker?"

"Who else?"

"We didn't rob him, we borrowed the money, he'll get the whole thing, we explained it to him."

"If you did it to me," Carlson said, "I'd say you robbed me."

They all thought about that for a minute, trying to imagine the situation reversed, and then Ross shrugged and said, "Okay, he thinks we robbed him. So what?"

"So maybe," Carlson said, "we shouldn't have left him alive."

Ross stared at him. "Meaning what?"

"Come on, Jerry, you know what I'm saying. If we're going to rob him, maybe we should go ahead and kill him."

Melander, firm about it, said, "Hal, we don't do that. We don't kill the people we work with. How could we *do* that?"

"Then there he is," Carlson said, "behind us, thinking how we robbed him. He didn't strike me as a let-it-ride kind of guy."

They thought about that awhile, going over their brief knowledge of Parker, and then Melander said, "We can keep in touch with him. We'll call him, time to time, let him know we're still gonna pay him, let him know it's gonna be all right."

"And make sure he's in place," Carlson said.

"That, too," Melander agreed.

When Tom Hurley had bowed out of the bank job and suggested Parker to take his place, he'd given them a way to make contact, if they had to. There was a phone number, and they should ask for Mr. Willis. But they shouldn't start off with that call, they should wait for him to make the first move, to let them know he was interested. As it happened, he'd done everything with that first move, so they hadn't had to use the Mr. Willis number, but now they could.

Except, four days later, with their freshly installed telephone at the estate in Palm Beach, when they tried that number there was no answer. They had a go at it on and off for three days, and then Carlson said, "He's following us."

Melander didn't like that. He walked around the empty living room, with the out-of-tune piano shoved into a corner, and he glared out at the terrace and the ocean and all the beautiful weather he was supposed to be enjoying instead of that icy northern shit, and he didn't like it at all. "We left the son of a bitch alive," he complained.

"Like I been saying," Carlson pointed out.

147

"We left the son of a bitch alive," Melander insisted, "so he'd know we were good for it, he can count on us, we'll come through. Not so he could follow us around and make trouble. We're busy here, we got a lot on our minds, we don't need this shit."

"Like I been saying," Carlson said.

"Jesus, Hal," Melander said, "what made you so fucking bloodthirsty all of a sudden? You never wanted to go around popping people before."

"I don't want to this time," Carlson said. "It just seems to me, before we did what we did, we should have thought it through a little more."

"Well, we didn't," Melander said, "and I don't see what more fucking *thought* was gonna do about it. We did what we had to do, what we agreed we had to do, and we did it and it's done and I swear to God, Hal, I want you out of my fucking face on this topic."

"I'm just saying," Carlson said.

"I *hear* you saying, and I'm *tired* of hearing you fucking saying, you follow me?"

Ross, speaking quietly as though in a room with some possibly dangerous dogs, said, "Maybe what we should do is go there."

They stopped glaring at each other to frown at Ross. Melander said, "Go where?"

"Where that phone number is," Ross said. "With a phone number, you can always get an address."

Melander, feeling belligerent toward everybody, said, "Go there and do what? What's the purpose?"

"Maybe there's something there tells us where he is," Ross said, still being very mild. "Or how to get in touch with him. And he's supposed to have a woman there, too, maybe she knows where he is. Or maybe she should come stay with us awhile to make sure Parker doesn't get to be too much."

"The woman," Melander said, nodding, losing his belligerence. "That's a good idea."

"I don't know about that," Carlson said. "Maybe that just makes it worse. First we rob him, then we kidnap his lady friend, maybe he's gonna—"

Exasperated, Melander said, "Why do you keep worrying about how *he's* gonna take it? Whose side are you *on?*"

"Mine," Carlson said.

Ross said, "Let's go take a look at the house."

So they did, driving up the east coast to the still-icy North, and the house was in northwest New Jersey, seventy miles from New York, on a lake where most of the houses were seasonal, still shut up for the winter. The house the Mr. Willis phone number led to, behind a rural mailbox that said "Willis" on the side, was small, part gray stone and part brown shingles, with an attached two-car garage. It was surrounded by trees and brush, and it was empty.

People lived here. There was much evidence of the woman, less evidence of the man, who had to be Parker. They found three guns stashed in the house, one clipped under the living room sofa, one clipped under the bed, and one in a sliding wood panel in the garage, next to the kitchen door, just above the button to operate the overhead garage door. That last was the one that got to Carlson. He could see it:

the guy makes an innocent turn to push that button, open or close the overhead door, and turns back with an S&W Chiefs Special .38 in his hand.

They could see that the woman had packed, and probably for an extended stay. But there was nothing to show where she'd gone, no travel agent's itinerary, no notes about airline connections, nothing. There was nothing at all about Parker; his footprint was not deep in this house.

They stayed four days in the house, finding a couple of diners and a supermarket not too many miles away, waiting to see if anybody showed up or if there was a phone call. If Parker phoned, looking for his woman, they'd talk to him, see if they could cool him out, discuss it with him.

But nothing happened, no calls, no visits, and after four days Melander couldn't stand it anymore. "*And* it's fucking cold," he said. "This isn't where I was gonna be right now."

Carlson said, "We aren't doing anything here except act like jerk-offs."

Melander, who'd been thinking the same thing, didn't like the thought when he heard it expressed. "Jerk-offs? What are you talking about?"

"We're sitting around here," Carlson told him, "waiting for people who aren't here and aren't gonna be here and in fact are probably themselves in Palm Beach."

"Getting warm," Ross said.

"Fuck it," Melander said. "Nobody's coming here, let's go back."

"Like I said," Carlson said.

They didn't want Parker to know they'd been there, in case he did happen to drop by before the Clendon job went down, so they put everything back the way they'd found it, including restashing the guns. There was a late snowstorm, which delayed them another day and got Melander's back up even more, and then they drove south, grousing at one another most of the way. They usually got along together, but the wait this time was getting to them, and the complication of Parker just made everything worse.

They got back to the estate in Palm Beach at almost midnight and went through switching on lights, echoing through the empty rooms, all of them looking for signs of Parker's presence, but none of them saying so. They met again in the kitchen and Ross said, "No change."

"Exactly like we left it," Carlson said.

Melander opened the refrigerator and got out three beers. "Well, wherever he is," he said, "at least he hasn't been here."

151

2

The funny thing is, she showed that condo two days later, the place where Daniel Parmitt—as if that was his name—told her about the three men who'd cheated him and who were going to steal Mrs. Miriam Hope Clendon's jewels. And the funnier thing is, Mr. and Mrs. Hochstein from Trenton, New Jersey, loved the condo, didn't want to haggle at all, didn't want to look at a thousand other places, loved the Bromwich, wanted to close right this second. The first place she showed them, and they were hooked, they were hers, which has never happened in the entire history of real estate. It was a sign.

Lord knows she needed a sign. Leslie hadn't heard from Parmitt since their discussion at the condo, and she would dearly love to know what was going on, but knew better than to call him and ask. He was a very private person, Mr. Daniel Parmitt. He would let you know how close you could get, and woe betide you if you crossed the line. She thought she understood Parmitt now, and how to deal with him. In a nutshell, he was everything that Gerry Mackenzie, her brain-dead ex, was supposed to have been but, it turned out, was not.

Gerry Mackenzie had been young Leslie Simons's first attempt to break out of the third-rate life she'd been dealt, growing up poor in West Palm, right next door to the ultra-rich, but never being quite poor enough to just throw in the towel. No; all the time she was growing up, her mother's favorite word had been "appearances." They had to keep up appearances, God knows why. They had to spend money for show, not for necessities. With a divorced mom who worked as a supermarket cashier and a slightly retarded older sister who was never going to be useful for anything and was never going to marry and become somebody else's burden, this meant for the young Leslie Simons an endless life of dreary pretense.

Gerry Mackenzie, a wholesale salesman for a big computer company, a glad-handing upbeat guy full of talk about the latest advances in the "industry," full of expertise and inside dirt, as though he himself were just on the verge of becoming the next software billionaire, had seemed just precisely the right prince to rescue Leslie Simons from the dungeon of her life. Only after she'd married him had she discovered that her mother had been an *amateur* when it came to keeping up appearances; Gerry was the

pro. It was all sparkle and flash with him, all salesman's hype, all toothy grins and pay-you-back-next-
week. It all came clear to her, one day in the second
year of the marriage, when she'd heard two of
Gerry's fellow salesmen talking about him, and one
said, "He comes on so great, but you know? He just
can't close."

She understood there were salesmen like that,
failed salesmen. (Not her, though; in real estate, she
was a shark for closing.) As a talker, Gerry Mackenzie
was a winner; as an earner, he was a flop. She got her
real estate agent's license during the marriage because *somebody* had to put food on the table, and after
a while she realized all she was getting out of this deal
was the opportunity to listen to Gerry gasbag all the
time. Home wasn't that great an alternative, but,
until something else came along, it was better than
Gerry. At least, she got to keep more of her earnings.

Was Daniel Parmitt the something else? Not to
marry, God knows, or even to sleep with, but to make
it possible for her to get *out* of here. On her own, this
time. Far away from Palm Beach, far away from
Florida entirely. Maybe the U.S. Virgin Islands, where
she could kick back in her own little place and let the
world go screw itself. On her own, strictly on her
own.

Which had been the other thing she'd learned
from marriage to Gerry Mackenzie: she didn't much
like sex. She never had, in the few times she'd tried it
with other people before Gerry, but then she'd always assumed it was because she and the guy didn't

know each other well enough or weren't compatible or whatever. With Gerry, they got to know each other very well, and Gerry certainly knew how to turn his salesman's charm to the question of sex, so that was one area in which she couldn't find him at fault.

No, it was her. She didn't think she was a lesbian, she'd never had any interest in that direction, either. She thought it was just that she didn't particularly need sex, so why go through with it? Messy, disorganized, and frequently embarrassing; the hell with it.

That was one of the good things about Daniel Parmitt; he didn't mistake her interest for a sexual one, and he was too focused on his own plans to have time for irrelevancies like sex with his local girl guide. There were moments when she thought it might be interesting to go to bed with him just once, just to see what it was like, but then she'd remember how cold his eyes had been the time he'd made her strip so he could be sure she wasn't tape-recording their conversation, and she knew that wasn't the look of somebody interested in her body. Even today, Gerry Mackenzie would give her a better time than that, if that's what she wanted.

It still surprised her that she'd been bold enough to go after Parmitt, before she'd known enough about him to know it was the right thing to do. Desperation, maybe, an antenna out frantically in search of a sign. Whatever it was, some instinct had grabbed her, that's all, and said, This guy will get you out of here. He'll get you out of here, and then he'll get out of your life. Grab him.

Would he? Would the people he was mad at really steal Mrs. Clendon's jewels and get away with it? Would Daniel Parmitt really take the jewels away from *them*? And would he really share some of the profit with her?

Maybe. Maybe. Maybe.

Did she have anything else going? Nothing. The commission on the Bromwich condo sale was very nice, but not what she needed. She'd known for a long time, you don't change your life on commissions. You need a score. Somewhere, somehow, a score.

Keep healthy, Daniel Parmitt, she thought. I've bet the farm on you.

3

Elvis Clagg saw the whole thing, from the beginning, right there in front of him. It was incredible. It was like a movie.

At twenty-three, Elvis Clagg wasn't the youngest member of the Christian Renewal Defense Force (CRDF), but he was the most recent recruit, having joined up only four months ago, bringing the CRDF's strength up to twenty-nine, its highest enlistment in more than fifteen years. Still, not one of those guys had ever themselves seen anything as amazing, and they were the first to admit it. Even Captain Bob, in his years in Nam, had never seen the like, and Captain Bob was over fifty years of age.

Captain Bob Hardawl himself had founded the CRDF not long after he'd come back to Florida from Nam and had seen that the niggers and kikes were about to take over everywhere from the forces of God, and that the forces of God could use some help from a fella equipped with infantryman training.

Armageddon hadn't struck yet, thank God, but you just knew that sooner or later it would. You could read all about it on the Internet, you could hear it in the songs of Aryan rock, you could see it in the news all around you, you could read it in all the books and magazines that Captain Bob insisted every member of the CRDF subscribe to and *read.*

That was an odd thing, too. Reading had always been tough for Elvis Clagg. It had been one of the reasons he'd dropped out of school at the very first opportunity and got that job at the sugar mill that paid shit and immediately gave him a bad cough like an old car. But now that he had stuff he *wanted* to read, stuff he *liked* to read, why, turned out, he was a natural at it.

They oughta figure that out in the schools. Quit giving the kids all that *Moby-Dick* shit and give them *The Protocols of Zion,* and you're gonna have you some heavy-duty readers.

But the point is, with all the reading everybody'd done, and all the sights that everybody'd seen—and three of the CRDF troopers had done time up at Raiford, so you know they're not exactly pansies— still and all, nobody had ever seen anything like this.

The entire troop of twenty-nine, Captain Bob Hardawl commanding, was deep in the Everglades on maneuvers, keeping up their tracking skills, learning jungle infiltration, when they heard the car. There was a road over there, of course, they'd just marched out on it, but you never heard a *car* on that road, it didn't go anywhere. Just to some fallen-down shacks used to belong to alligator hunters or maybe even older, egret hunters, from when the fancy ladies up north liked to wear egret feathers in their hats. So why was a car coming this way?

Billy Joe, one of the more excitable members of the group, called, "Captain Bob, interlopers! Suppose they're Feds?"

Feds! The deadly battle with government lawmen, always a possibility, always the threat out there waiting. Was it here now? Elvis searched the sky, clutching his Uzi to his chest, but he saw no black helicopters.

"Easy, boys," Captain Bob called to his line of men, and held his Colt .45 automatic up in the air to signal they should stand where they were. The rest of them all carried Uzis adapted to fire only one shot at a time, to make them legal, which of course would be unadapted in a flat second once Armageddon started, but Captain Bob, as the leader, was the only one with a side arm.

"I see it!" Jack Ray called, and then they all saw it. A white utility vehicle, it was, looked foreign, moving along the road toward the curve where they themselves had turned off into the glades not five minutes ago.

Captain Bob gestured downward with the .45, and

they all crouched, twenty-nine men in camouflage uniforms with greasepaint and Off! on their faces. In a minute, the car would go around that curve and on out of sight.

And then it happened, astonishingly. Instead of slowing, the car abruptly *speeded up,* and its right front door opened, on the side away from the CRDF, and a man fell or jumped out of it.

The car yawed this way and that, brakes on hard, tires slipping on the muddy road, and the *near* side rear door opened and *another* man came rolling out, and this one was clutching a rifle in vertical position against his chest, exactly the way Captain Bob had taught the CRDF to do, if they ever had to bail out of something big, moving fast.

The car slewed around, the first man started to his feet as though to run off into the glades, and damn if the second man didn't come up on one knee, aim, and shoot the first man in the back. *Whang!* Down he went; son of a bitch!

And tried to get up. They could see him struggle as the man with the rifle got up and walked toward him and the white car finally came to a stop, and the driver stuck his head out to yell something to the shooter.

Captain Bob started yelling then, too: "Hey! Hold on there! You men stop there!"

But they couldn't hear him, or they were concentrating too much to pay attention, so the whole CRDF watched the rifleman kick the man he'd shot to roll him down into the water, and then take aim to shoot him again up close.

That was when Captain Bob fired his side arm into the air to attract their attention.

Which it did. The driver of the car and the rifleman both turned to stare at the crouching CRDF, and then, quick as a wink, the rifleman whipped up his rifle and fired at *them*!

A fella named Hoby that had bad teeth and was three guys to Elvis's left flopped backward like a cut line of wash. Just back and down.

The truth is, if it wasn't for the CRDF, Elvis personally would have panicked at that point and gone running like a greyhound into the glades. But there *was* the CRDF, and he was part of it, and he stuck.

"Two lines!" called Captain Bob while the rifleman fired again and a fella named Floyd did the back-flop thing, and the remaining twenty-six troopers, with Captain Bob tall at their right end, quickly formed into two broad lines facing the foe. The front rank dropped to one knee.

"Front rank!" yelled Captain Bob as the rifleman suddenly took off running toward the car. "The vehicle!"

Which meant the rear rank, which included Elvis, was to take out the rifleman. Okay. Not much leading at this distance. Hands steady as a rock.

"Fire!"

Thirteen bullets went into the driver and thirteen bullets went into the rifleman.

The CRDF's first military engagement. They'd

taken two casualties out of a force of twenty-nine, and the opposing force was completely wiped out. As far as Elvis Clagg was concerned, the CRDF had just kicked ass.

4

Dear," said Alice Prester Young, "do we know a Daniel Parmitt?"

Jack Young looked up from his *Wall Street Journal* to smile across the breakfast table at his bride. "Who, dear?"

"Parmitt, Daniel Parmitt. It says here he's staying at the Breakers."

"It says where?"

"In the *Herald.*"

Jack Young's smile was the soul of patience. "Dear," he said, "why is Mr. Parmitt in the *Herald*?"

"Because he was shot. Not expected to live."

"Shot!" Jack's surprise was genuine. "Why would we know anybody that was shot?"

"Well, it says he's staying at the Breakers, so I'm wondering if he's here for the ball."

"Well, if he's been shot," Jack said, "he isn't likely to come to the ball."

"No, dear, but I was just wondering."

"If we knew him," Jack said.

"Yes, dear," she said, although by now she had realized that wasn't the actual question at all. It wasn't did *they* know this Daniel Parmitt, it was did *she* know him. Jack wouldn't be likely to know anybody from *her* past, would he?

This was her first season at the beach as Alice Prester Young, after having been Alice Prester Habib forever. Eleven years; hard to believe. Before that, somebody else, before that, somebody else, who even remembers anymore?

It was very nice to bring an attractive new husband to the beach for the season, introduce him around, let the biddies turn green with envy. And it was especially nice to know that one could still look *all right* on the arm of such a husband. One didn't look exactly like a girl anymore, but one certainly did look *all right.*

Particularly the body. Between the doctors and the dietitians and the personal trainers, it was possible, though not easy, to keep a hard youthful body forever, to offer an attentive young husband something interesting and responsive in bed. The face could be kept smooth and attractive, but never quite exactly girlish. The softnesses and roundnesses of youth can never be recaptured on the face, so the best you can hope for in that department is angular, slightly hollow, good looks, more striking than beautiful. But who could complain? At sixty-seven, to have a striking face above the body of a twenty-year-old wasn't bad. And a twenty-six-year-old brand-new husband.

Why had she stayed so long with Habib?

Jack broke into her thoughts by saying, "Somebody shot this fellow at the Breakers?"

"No, dear, he's *staying* at the Breakers. They kidnapped him—"

"What!"

"—and took him into the Everglades and shot him there."

"Who? Why?"

"Apparently it was a case of mistaken identity. They were professional killers, and whoever they were supposed to kill they took this man Parmitt by mistake."

"Now, that's what I call bad luck," Jack said, and laughed. "And besides that, he doesn't get to go to the ball."

"Oh, that reminds me, the auction," she said. "Dear, would you be a dear?"

"Of course," he said. He'd been just as attentive when he'd been an insurance company claims adjuster and they'd met after that silly automobile accident in Short Hills. Now, his bright blue eyes eager, he said, "What do you need, dear?"

"My albums," she said. "Not last year's, but the two years before that."

"Coming up," he said. He rose, smiled, folded his *Journal*, put it on the chair, and went off to her study, leaving her in the cool and quiet breakfast room, all

165

pink and gold, with its view over the sea grape at the limitless ocean.

In a minute he was back with the two albums she'd asked for, both big thick volumes with padded pastel covers and glassine sheets within, inside which, every year, Alice inserted all photos and social-page stories involving her. Which meant, naturally, that most of the other important Beachers would also be seen in the various photos.

"What I'm looking for . . . ," Alice said, pushing her coffee cup aside and riffling through the first album, "what I want . . . is . . . yes! There, see it?"

She had found a newspaper photo showing the three co-chairs of a charity ball from two years ago, the last year Miriam Hope Clendon had still been active in society. The three overdressed women were lined up in a row to face the camera, Miriam in the center, of course, being the grande dame, with Helena Stockworth Fritz on her right and Alice on her left. But this time it wasn't at herself Alice wanted to look, nor even at the rather portly and snout-faced Miriam, but at the necklace around Miriam's neck, on which she tapped a mauve false fingernail.

Jack leaned attentively over her shoulder, smiling vaguely at the photo. "What am I looking at, dear?"

"The necklace, Miriam's necklace. *That's* what I'm going to bid on. I've had my eye on that necklace ever since I first met Miriam, oh, some years ago."

"It's beautiful," Jack said, and in his eye was the glint, though Alice didn't see it, of a man looking at a necklace he expects to inherit someday.

"We have to do a sealed bid on *something* to get into the auction," she said with satisfaction, "and *that's* what I'm after, and I believe I'll get it."

"Won't other people bid for it?"

"Not for long," she said. "It's extremely valuable, you know."

"Yes, it looks it."

"*Most* people, *I* believe," Alice said, "will just go for the baubles, because they won't want to spend an awful lot of money this late in the season. Just so they take home some little thing. But *I* will bid on this necklace, and I'll bid low, and because it's so valuable it won't come on the block until very late, when everybody else will already have their little something, and I wouldn't be surprised if I get it for my opening bid."

"How clever you are, Alice," Jack said, and patted her shoulder before he went back around to his seat and his *Wall Street Journal*.

She continued to smile at the necklace in the photo. "What a coup," she said. "To get that necklace cheap, and to wear it on *every* occasion." Like all very wealthy women, Alice had strange cold pockets of miserliness. Her eyes shone as she looked across the table at Jack. "It will be an absolute *steal*," she said.

5

Trooper Sergeant Jake Farley of the Snake River County sheriff's department had never seen anything like *this* before. Four dead, one dying, all questions, no answers. Nothing but frustration, all the way around.

Starting with blowhard "Captain" Robert Hardawl and his collection of retards and misfits that he called the Christian Renewal Defense Force. Hardawl and his scruffy gang had been a thorn in Sergeant Farley's side for years, always threatening violence, never quite going far enough to get themselves busted up and put away where they couldn't be an offense to decent law enforcement people anymore.

Two, three times a year, Farley would sit down with Agent Mobley from the Miami office of the FBI to discuss the various hate groups and paramilitary

168

loonies wandering around these swamps, and Hardawl and his crowd were always prominent in that discussion. And now they've gone ahead at last and killed two men, and there wasn't one blessed thing Farley could do about it, because, goddammit, it was self-defense, and Hardawl had his own two dead bodies to prove it, shot with the same firearm that shot Daniel Parmitt.

Who was another frustration. Who the hell was he? Some rich fella from Texas, that's all, spending part of the winter in Palm Beach, grabbed up by two professional killers from Baltimore either because somebody wanted Daniel Parmitt dead—to inherit his money, maybe?—or because they got the wrong man.

Being unable to ask Gowan and Vavrina who hired them because they'd been all shot to shit by Hardawl's people, and being unable to ask Parmitt who might want him dead because he damn near *was* dead, unconscious and slowly slipping away, meant Farley had nobody to ask anything except Hardawl and his pack of losers, who didn't know anything. It was enough to make a man bite his badge.

Four days. The Baltimore police and the Maryland state police had shared all the information they had on Gowan and Vavrina, which was a lot, but didn't include the name of their most recent employer. The San Antonio police had passed on to Farley what they could find out about Parmitt, which wasn't much: never been in trouble with the law, owned a house in a nice part of town, was loved by his bankers. The Breakers had sent along Parmitt's possessions from the hotel, which consisted mainly of resort wear. He traveled with his birth certificate, which was about the only oddity Farley had seen in it all.

Snake River County didn't get much of what Jake Farley thought of as big-city crime, meaning gangland killings, professional armed robbery, that sort of thing, but what they did get was all his; he was the one man in the sheriff's department who'd been through the FBI courses and the state CID courses and had even been sent off with the help of federal funding for a couple of courses at John Jay College of Criminal Justice up in New York City; *that* had been an experience.

But even that hadn't prepared him for this situation. He had the victim, he had the perps—far too many perps, in fact—he had the weapons, he had every damn thing, and yet he couldn't have known less about what was going on if he was a brand-new baby boy. So here he was on the fourth day of the so-called investigation, seated at his corner desk in the bullpen at the sheriff's department, trying to think of somebody to call, when his phone rang. He gave it a jaundiced look before he answered: "Farley."

"Meany here, Sarge."

Meany was the deputy on duty at the hospital, to report any change in Parmitt's condition, so this was the one phone call Farley had definitely not wanted: "So he's dead, huh?"

"Well, no, sir. The reason I'm calling, he woke up."

Farley's back lost its slump: "What?"

"And there's a woman here to see him."

"A woman? For Parmitt?"

"Yes, sir. Read about it in the *Miami Herald,* she said, said she had to talk to him."

"Not before me," Farley said. "Hold her there, keep him awake, I'll be right over."

The woman was a good-looking blonde of about forty with some heft to her; the kind of woman Farley was attracted to, in his off-duty hours. In fact, the kind of woman he was married to, which meant his off-duty hours were few and far between.

And this wasn't one of them. He entered the waiting room, saw Meany standing there, saw the woman rise from one of the green vinyl sofas, and crossed to her to say, "Trooper Sergeant Farley, sheriff's department." He did not offer to shake hands.

She said, "I'm Leslie Mackenzie."

"And you're a friend of Daniel Parmitt's."

"Yes. I'd really like to talk with him."

"So would I," Farley told her. "Rank gets its privileges here. I go first, then we'll see if the doctor says it's all right for you."

"I'll wait," she said, "however long it takes."

So she was *that* kind of friend, a little more than a friend but not quite family. Farley said, "You can probably tell me more about him. We'll talk in a while."

"All right," she said.

171

Farley turned away, giving Meany a quick frown and headshake that meant don't-let-her-leave, then went out and down the hall toward Parmitt's room.

This was only the second time he'd visited Parmitt, the first being shortly after the man was brought in, when visiting him was nothing but a waste of time. Parmitt was a real wreck then, shot, nearly drowned, and some of his ribs caved in.

What had happened was, he'd been shot in the back, the bullet passing through his body, hitting nothing vital, missing the spine by an inch, nicking a rib on the way out. Then the killer rolled him into the water, unconscious, and by the time the war with Hardawl's crew was over, the fella was drowned.

One thing you had to give Hardawl credit for—and Farley hated to have to admit it—he did give his people good training, including drowning rescues and CPR. They knew enough to lay the man on his stomach, head to the side, somebody's finger in his mouth to keep him from swallowing his tongue, while somebody else did some heavy bearing-down on his back, in slow rhythmic movements, to get the water out and start the process of breathing again. This can crack ribs, the way it did this time, and this time was even worse, because that was rough treatment for a torso that had just had a bullet pass through it, but Hardawl had realized there was no choice. If you don't get the water out, the man's dead anyway.

Well, he was a tough son of a bitch, Parmitt, and he survived the drowning rescue just the way he survived the shot and the drowning, but when they brought him in and Farley got that one gander at him, he sure did look like a candidate for the last rites. So what would he look like now?

Not that much better. They had the upper half of the bed cranked partway up, to make it easier for him to breathe, and his entire torso was swathed in bandages. His eyes were deep-set and ringed with dark shadow, his cheeks were sunken, and that snaky little mustache looked like somebody's idea of a bad joke, painted on him as though he were a face in an advertising poster. His arms, held away from his body because of the thicknesses of wrapping around his chest, were above the blanket, lying limp, the big hands half-curled in his lap. He was breathing slowly through his mouth, and when he saw Farley the look in his eyes was dull and without curiosity.

A white-coated intern was in the room, looking at the patient, just standing there, and he turned to say, "Sheriff."

Farley never bothered to correct people's use of titles; he was in the tan uniform of the sheriff's department, so if they wanted to call him Sheriff or Deputy or Officer or Trooper or anything else, he knew it didn't mean much more than *hello*, so why fret it. He said, "How's our patient?"

"Conscious, but barely. I understand you want to question him."

"More than you can imagine."

173

"Try to make it short, and if he starts to get upset, you'll have to stop."

"I understand," Farley said "I've been at bedsides before."

There were two chrome and vinyl chairs in the room. Farley brought one over to the side of the bed and sat on it, so he and Parmitt were now at the same height. "Mr. Parmitt," he said.

The eyes slowly moved to focus on him, but Parmitt didn't turn his head. Maybe he couldn't. But it was a strange gesture; here the man was the victim, nearly dead, weak as a kitten, but in that eye movement he suddenly looked to Farley extremely dangerous.

Which was foolish, of course. Farley said, "How do you feel, Mr. Parmitt?"

"Where am I?" It was just a whisper, no strength in it at all. The intern, at the foot of the bed, probably couldn't make out the words.

So Parmitt gets to ask the questions first. Okay, Farley could go along with that. He said, "You're in the Elmer Neuman Memorial Hospital, Snake River, Florida."

"Florida." He whispered it like a word he didn't know, and then his brow wrinkled and he said, "Why am I in Florida?"

"On vacation, like everybody else," Farley told him. "Don't you remember? You're staying at the Breakers, up in Palm Beach."

"I live in San Antonio," Parmitt whispered. "I

was . . . I was driving to my club. Was I in an accident?"

And this was something Farley had seen before, too. In bad accidents, or after bad scenes of violence, often the victims don't remember any of the events leading up to the trauma. Later on it would come back to them, maybe, but not right away.

Unfortunate. Farley could see there was no point questioning the man now, he didn't remember enough, and if he were told somebody out there was trying to kill him it just might put him into shock. So he said, "Yeah, you were in a kind of accident. You're still getting over it, Mr. Parmitt. We'll talk again when you feel better."

"Was I driving?"

Farley had to lean close to understand the man. "What? No, sir, you weren't driving."

"I have . . . an excellent safety record."

"I'm sure you do, Mr. Parmitt," Farley said, and got to his feet, and said, "We'll talk later."

Leslie Mackenzie was again seated on the vinyl sofa. She started to rise when Farley entered, but he patted the air, saying, "Stay there, Ms. Mackenzie, we'll sit and talk."

He sat at the other end of the sofa, half-turned to face her, and said, "You're a friend of Mr. Parmitt's. Known him long?"

"Only a few weeks," she said, and opened her purse on her lap. "I'm a real estate agent in Palm

Beach," she explained, and produced her business card. "My card."

He accepted it, looked at it, tucked it away in his shirt pocket, looked at her.

She said, "Mr. Parmitt was thinking of buying in Palm Beach, and I showed him some places, and we started to date. In fact, we had an appointment—to look at a house, not a date—and when he didn't show up, I didn't know what to think. Then I read about the—what is it? attempted murder—in the *Herald,* and I came here as soon as I could get away."

Farley saw no reason to disbelieve the woman. She was who she claimed to be, and her relationship with Parmitt sounded about right. In fact, her hurrying down here all the way from Palm Beach suggested to Farley she'd had some idea of her friendship with Parmitt blossoming into something more. She wouldn't be the first real estate woman in the world to wind up marrying a rich client. They walk into all those bedrooms together, and finally something clicks.

Well, more power to her. Farley said, "I have to tell you, Ms. Mackenzie, at the moment he doesn't remember much. Doesn't remember the shooting at all, doesn't remember coming to Florida. Right now, he might not remember you."

The slow smile she gave him was startlingly powerful. "Trooper," she said, "or Sergeant. What do I call you?"

"Sergeant," he said, pleased and grateful that she made the effort to get it right.

"Sergeant," she said, "if Daniel Parmitt doesn't re-member *me,* I'm not half the woman I think I am."

Farley always found himself growing awkward and foolish when a woman talked dirty in front of him. He blinked, and tried a half smile, and said, "Well, you can go and have a word with him if you like. The only thing, the doctor said, try not to get him excited."

She laughed. After she left, he could feel the blush still hot on his face.

6

Leslie was shocked by the look of him. She hadn't known what exactly to expect, but not this. He was like some powerful motor that had been switched off, inert, no longer anything at all. The look in his eyes was dull, the hands curled on his lap seemed dead.

Would he remember her? It had seemed to her that the best way to handle that sheriff sergeant was to give him the idea she and Daniel had something sexual going, because if that wasn't the reason for her being here, what *was* the reason? Also, she could see that he was one of those men made uneasy by talk about sex from a woman, and it would probably be a good idea to keep him off balance a bit.

But in fact, if Daniel was as harmed as he looked, maybe he really wouldn't remember her, maybe her imprint wasn't that deep with him.

There was a white-coated intern in the room, seated in a corner on a chrome and vinyl chair, writing on a form on a clipboard. He nodded at Leslie and said, "You can talk with him, but not for long. You'll have to get close, though, he can't speak above a whisper."

"Thank you."

A second chair stood over beside the bed. Reluctant, wishing now she hadn't come, that she'd merely telephoned to find out what his situation was— though then she wouldn't have found out what she needed to know about the three men—she went over to that chair and sat down and said, "Daniel."

His eyes had followed her as she crossed the room, and now he whispered, "What day is it?" The whisper was hoarse, rusty, and barely carried across the space between them.

She leaned closer. "Monday," she said.

"Four days," he whispered.

"Four days? What do you mean?"

"Auction."

"What? You aren't still thinking about *that*."

He ignored her, following his own lines of thought, saying, "How do you know I'm here?"

"It was in the *Herald*. You were shot and the people who shot you were killed by—"

"*Herald*? Newspaper?"

"Yes. On Saturday. I couldn't get here till now."

"Leslie," he whispered, "you've got to get me out of here."

Now she was whispering, too, almost as inaudible

as him, because of the intern, who was paying them no attention. She leaned closer yet to whisper, "You can't leave! You can't even move!"

"I can do better than they think. If I'm in the paper, somebody else could come to finish me."

This was the subject she really wanted to talk about, and the main reason for her trip here. The three robbers. She whispered, "It's the people you want to steal from, isn't it? Do they know about me?"

"Different. Not them."

That was a surprise. She'd taken it for granted it was the three men planning the robbery who'd discovered Daniel and had him shot, and quite naturally she'd wondered if they also knew about *her.* She whispered, "There's somebody *else?* Who?"

"Don't know. Don't care. Just so I get out of here. Leslie."

"What?"

"The longer I'm here, the more the cops are gonna wonder about me. My background, my name. And I can't have them take my prints."

"Oh."

She sat back, considering him. He was really in a terrible situation, wasn't he? Battered, weak, being pursued by killers he didn't seem even to know, trapped in this hospital with police all around, and now it turns out his fingerprints would lead the police to something dangerous in his background. And the only person in the whole entire world who could help him was her.

This time, she wasn't surprised by him, she was surprised by herself. She felt suddenly very strong. Her emotion toward Daniel Parmitt wasn't love or sex, but it *was* tender. It was almost, oddly, maternal. Now she was the strong one, she was the one who could help. And she *wanted* to help; she wanted him to know that when he asked the question, she would be there with the answer.

She leaned even closer to him, one forearm on the bed as she gazed into his eyes, seeing they weren't really as dull as he pretended. She whispered, "How bad off are you, really? Can you walk?"

"I don't know. I can try."

"In the paper, it said you weren't expected to live. Won't that make these other people wait?"

"Awhile."

"All right," she said. "I don't know how I'll do it, but I'll do it. I'll see what I can arrange, and I'll come back tomorrow."

He watched her leave. The intern sat in the corner, writing.

7

Mrs. Helena Stockworth Fritz was an extremely busy woman, never more so than since the death of dear Miriam Hope Clendon. There were the foundation boards to sit on, the press interviews, the arrangements for the charity balls, the lunches, the shopping, the phone calls with friends far and near, the yoga, the aura therapist, the constant planning for this or that event; and now the auction of dear Miriam's jewelry, right here at Seascape.

And not merely on the grounds, but inside the house as well. Most times, charity occasions at Seascape were held out on the side lawn and the terrace above the seawall overlooking the Atlantic, but this time it was necessary to have the jewelry on display, and to have the auctioneer where all the attendees could see and hear him, and so it was necessary to open the ballroom at Seascape with its broad line of tall French doors leading out to the terrace and the famous view. So in the middle of all this frenzy of activity, the last thing Mrs. Fritz needed was the delivery, three days early, of the musicians' amplifiers.

Jeddings came with the news, to the parlor where Mrs. Fritz was deep in concentration on her flower arranging. Jeddings looked worried, as she always did, and clutched her inevitable clipboard to her narrow chest as she said, "Mrs. Fritz, deliverymen at the gate."

"Delivery? Delivering what?"

"They say the amplifiers for the musicians."

"Musicians? We aren't having musicians tonight."

"No, Mrs. Fritz, for the auction."

The auction. Yes, there would be music that night, of course, dancing and the drinking of champagne before the auction began, to loosen up the attendees. But that wasn't till Friday, the day after the ball at the Breakers when the jewelry would first be publicly displayed, and today was only Tuesday. "What on earth are they delivering amplifiers *now* for?"

"I don't know, Mrs. Fritz, they say this is the only time they can do it."

"Let me see these people."

Mrs. Fritz accompanied Jeddings to the vestibule, which was what they called the very well-equipped office at the front of the house, near the main door. Jeddings and two clerks operated from here, helping to keep all of Mrs. Fritz's many charities and social events and other activities on track, and the video intercom to the front entrance was here.

Mrs. Fritz stopped in front of the monitor to frown at the TV image there. Once again, as always, that stray thought came and went: Why can't these things be in color like everything else? But that, of course, wasn't the point. The point was that, stopped just outside the gate, half blocking traffic, was a small nondescript dark van, containing two men. The driver was hard to see, but the passenger, a burly man with a thick shock of wavy black hair, was half-leaned out his open window, where he'd been speaking on the intercom and was now awaiting a reply.

"Tell him," Mrs. Fritz said, "this is a very inconvenient time."

"Yes, Mrs. Fritz."

Jeddings sat at the desk, picked up the phone, and said, "Mrs. Fritz says this is a very inconvenient time." Then she depressed the loudspeaker button so Mrs. Fritz could hear the reply.

Which was polite and amiable, but not helpful. Mrs. Fritz watched the burly man smile as he said, "I'm sorry about that. I don't like no dissatisfied customers, but they give us this stuff and said deliver it today, and we got no place to keep it. We got no insurance for this stuff. These amplifiers, I dunno how much they cost, I don't wanna be responsible for these things."

Jeddings covered the phone's mouthpiece with a hand and turned her worried face toward Mrs. Fritz. "We could store them in a corner of the ballroom, Mrs. Fritz. They wouldn't be in the way."

Mrs. Fritz didn't like it, but she could see it was

simply going to be one of those inconveniences one had to put up with, so grumpily she said, "Very well. But I don't want to be tripping over them."

"Oh, no, Mrs. Fritz," Jeddings promised, and spoke into the phone: "Very well. Come in." And she pushed the button to open the outer doors.

Mrs. Fritz could see that the burly man said something else, but this time Jeddings had not pressed the loudspeaker button. "That's fine," Jeddings said, and hung up, and the big wooden doors out there began to roll open.

Mrs. Fritz said, "What did he say?"

"He said thank you, Mrs. Fritz."

"Polite, in any event. *That's* a rarity."

"Yes, Mrs. Fritz."

"I'll come along, see where you intend to place these things."

"Yes, Mrs. Fritz."

They went out to the front hallway, with the double curving staircase and the pink marble floor, cool in the hottest weather, and Jeddings opened the front door as the van came crunching across the gravel around the curving drive to roll past the entrance and then back up. "Shore Fire Delivery" was not very professionally printed in white on the doors.

The two men got out and came around to the rear of the van, the burly man smiling up at Mrs. Fritz and saying, "Afternoon, ma'am. Sorry about the inconvenience."

"That's all right," she said, to be gracious, though everyone present was well aware it was not all right.

The driver was a smaller man, skinny, sharp-featured, with very large ears. The two were dressed in normal workman's clothes, dark shapeless pants and T-shirts, the burly man's advertising beer, the driver's advertising the Miami Dolphins.

Why did the underclass so enjoy turning itself into billboards?

When the van doors were opened, two very large black boxes became visible inside, along with a hand truck, which the burly man brought out first. Then the two of them wrestled one of the boxes out of the van and onto the hand truck, and Mrs. Fritz and Jeddings backed out of the doorway as the two men thumped the thing up the broad stairs and into the house. It had the usual dials and switches across the top, and black cloth across the front, and the brand name Magno in chrome letters attached to the front near the bottom.

Jeddings led the way through the house, the burly man wheeling the hand truck ahead of himself, the driver walking beside him with one hand on the amplifier to keep it from falling over, and Mrs. Fritz brought up the rear, looking to be sure their wheels didn't hurt the parquet.

Fortunately, the placement of the display tables for the jewelry and the auctioneer's dais had already been determined, and tables and dais were now all in place. Mrs. Fritz had not wanted to worry about details like *that* on the day. So they'd be able to place the amplifiers where they would not be underfoot while the rest of the preparations were being made, and would not be in a spot where it turned out something else had to be put.

It was the burly man, in fact, who suggested where to put the amplifiers. Pointing to the corner farthest from the display tables, he said, "Ma'am, if we put them over there, I don't think they'd bother you."

"Good," she said, "do that, then."

They did, and repeated the operation with the second amplifier, placing it beside the first. Then they wheeled their hand truck back to the front door, the burly man smiled his way through another set of apologies—Mrs. Fritz was gracious again—and then she went into the vestibule to watch on the monitor as the van drove away and the big doors were shut once more.

Jeddings said, "Mrs. Fritz, I'll have staff put a tablecloth over them—you won't even notice them."

"Good. You do that."

Jeddings did do that, and the amplifiers disappeared under a snowy damask tablecloth, and nobody gave them another thought.

8

I don't want to," Loretta whined.

Loretta always whined, but her whines were different, sometimes merely expressing her general attitude toward life, other times standing for specific emotions, like anger or fear or petulance or weariness. This one right now was her bullheaded stubborn whine, with that extra twang in it, and rumbles of mutiny.

Time to put a stop to that. Leslie turned to her mother, across the table. "Mom," she said, "I don't ask much."

Her mother, Laurel, put down her fork and frowned deeply, her leathery beige face creasing like a supermarket paper bag, because she never liked to have to mediate disputes between her daughters, between Leslie the quick one and Loretta the slow one, slightly retarded, badly overweight, never quite grasping what was going on.

The three were seated together at the dinner table on Wednesday evening, and Leslie knew she had to force the issue now because tomorrow would be the last day to try to get Daniel Parmitt out of the hospital. She'd thought and she'd thought, and this was the only idea she'd come up with for a way to slip him out of there, and it just simply required Loretta's cooperation. No other choice.

But her mother was making trouble, as well. "Leslie," she said, "if only you'd tell us *why* you want to do this."

Which, naturally, she could not. But why should she have to? *She* was the provider in the family, *she* was the one who held it all together, how dare they question her? "Mom," she said, forcing herself to be calm and reasonable, "this man is a friend. Not a lover, it's not like that, a friend. He's in trouble, and he asked me to help, and I'm going to help, and I need Loretta."

"I don't want to get in trouble," Loretta whined.

"You won't get in trouble," Leslie told her, not for the first time. "You just do what I say, and it'll be *easy.*"

"Mom," Loretta whined.

Leslie looked at her mother. "Or," she said, slow and deliberate, to let her mother know she was serious about this, "I could move out." She didn't mention, nor at this moment did she more than barely think about it, that if this all happened the way it was supposed to, she'd be moving out anyway.

Loretta looked stricken. She had only the vaguest idea what life would be like without Leslie in the house, but she understood it would be in some way horrible. Worse than now.

Their mother looked from one to the other. She sighed. She said, "Loretta, I think you have to do it."

Loretta lowered her head to aim her put-upon look at the food on her plate. Her mother turned to Leslie: "What time will you want to leave?"

"At four," Leslie said. "And it really will be easy, Mom. Nothing to it."

9

Alice Prester Young knew she was a herd animal, and enjoyed the knowledge, because the herd she moved with was the very *best* herd in all the world. For instance, here she was, at five-thirty on this Thursday afternoon, in her chauffeured Daimler, on her way to the bank with her new husband, the delicious Jack, to pick up just the *perfect* jewelry for tonight's pre-auction ball, and she knew when she arrived at the bank she would be surrounded by her own kind, chauffeured and cosseted women with attractive escorts, all coming to the bank (the only bank one could use, really) because this particular bank stayed open late whenever there was an important ball in town, just so the herd could come get its jewelry out of the safe-deposit boxes. And the bank would open again, later tonight, when the same herd left the ball and returned to redeposit their jewelry all over again.

The ritual of the bank was almost as enjoyable as the ritual of the ball itself, though shorter. The staff was quiet, methodical, servile without being obsequious. The herd cooed greetings to one another and exclaimed with pleasure over each other's choice of which pieces to wear to this special occasion. The mirrors that the bank had installed in the rooms outside the safe-deposit vault were very special mirrors, not clear like common mirrors but tinted the most delicate gray, so that when the ladies of the herd looked at themselves as they put on their jewelry, they did not see as many wrinkles or age spots or other flaws as a common mirror might unfeelingly display. The bank cared about the feelings of the herd, and Alice Prester Young liked that, too.

How was it phrased, in that little map and pamphlet the tourists could pick up? The people of Palm Beach were "those who feel they have earned the right to live well." Yes. Precisely. That's exactly how Alice felt. She had—somehow—earned the right to move with this plump and comfortable herd, to ride in the Daimler with her brand-new husband, to the beach, to the ball, to the bank.

Another glorious night!

Five-thirty. Trooper Sergeant Jake Farley sat in a side booth at Cindy's Luncheonette and drank coffee with FBI Agent Chris Mobley, a big spread-out Kentuckian with an easy grin and cold eyes. They were discussing, yet again, the wounded man from Texas, Daniel Parmitt.

"I just don't know where else to get at this thing from," Farley said. "The shooters are a blind alley, but every time I try to talk to Parmitt he gets all vague on me, can't remember a damn thing. I asked him would he mind if I bring in a hypnotist, and he said yeah he did, so here I am, still stuck."

Mobley said, "Why'd he nix the hypnotist?"

"Said he didn't like 'em, thought they were phony."

"If they're phony," Mobley said, "they can't do nothing to him."

"You can't reason with a man in a hospital bed," Farley said. "I've learned that a good long time ago. Man in a hospital bed feels sorry for himself and sore at the world. You can't reason with him."

Mobley sipped coffee and squinted toward the front of Cindy's and the street outside. "You think he's a wrong one somehow?"

Farley frowned at him. "How'd you mean?"

"Somebody shot him," Mobley pointed out. "Man gets shot, usually it means somebody had a reason. How come he don't know what the reason is?"

"He doesn't remember the last week at all," Farley said.

"Well, how about two weeks ago?" Mobley asked. "Wouldn't the people with a reason have a reason back that far?"

Farley frowned deeper at that. "You think he's fakin? Lyin? Stallin?"

"You've seen him, I haven't," Mobley said. "But the

193

man oughta know who's mad at him, oughta know at least that much."

"Mmm," Farley said, and frowned at his coffee.

"I tell you what," Mobley said. "Tomorrow, you run off a set of his prints, fax 'em to me in Miami, we'll check 'em up at SOG."

Farley thought that over and slowly nodded. "Couldn't hurt, I suppose," he said.

Six o'clock. Leslie drove south on Interstate 95, Loretta an unhappy lump on the passenger seat beside her. Loretta was already dressed in the long tan raincoat and the wide-brimmed straw hat with the pink ribbon, and she was staring mulishly out the windshield. She wouldn't look at Leslie and certainly wouldn't talk to her. Loretta would go along with the plan, because she had no choice and she knew it, but she was definitely in a grade-A snit.

Well, it didn't matter, just so she did her part. Everything was falling into place, starting with this car. Another rep at Leslie's firm, Gloria, was what is called a soccer mom, which meant she spent all her nonworking time transporting masses of small children and all their necessary gear to sub-teen sporting events. For this purpose, her second car was this Plymouth Voyager, with the middle line of seats removed and a ramp installed that could be angled out from the wide side door to accommodate wheeled trunks full of basketballs or hockey sticks or whatever was needed. Leslie had arranged to borrow this vehicle from Gloria for this afternoon and evening, explaining she had to take her sister to a complicated medical procedure that would leave her unable to walk for a few days, and now they were on their way.

She looked out ahead, far down the straight wide road, and said with surprise, "Well, *there's* something you don't see every day."

Loretta almost looked at Leslie, or asked what it was you don't see every day, but she caught herself in time and went on being a lump.

Leslie watched the fire engine down there, rolling north, moving very fast in the left lane, overtaking everything on the road. "It's a fire engine, Loretta," she said. "A great big red fire engine. See it? I wonder where it's going."

Loretta finally did focus on the fire engine, having to turn her head to keep watching it as they passed one another. She actually started to smile, but then became aware of Leslie observing her, and quickly frowned instead.

"I like fire engines," Leslie said, expecting no response and getting none.

"I like fire engines," Hal Carlson said as they high-balled north.

Seated beside him, Jerry Ross grinned. "What I like," he said, "is fire."

Seven-thirty. Mrs. Helena Stockworth Fritz was not part of the herd. She was, in fact, above the herd, as the whole world acknowledged, and that's why she did not, before each ball, pay a visit at the bank.

195

The late Mr. Fritz (munitions, oil, cargo ships, warehouses, all inherited) had, many years ago, during a spate of politically inspired financier kidnappings, installed a safe room in the middle of Seascape, which Mrs. Fritz still used for her most valuable valuables. The safe room was a concrete box, twelve feet square and eight feet high, built *under* the building, into the water table but sealed and dry. A dedicated phone line in stainless-steel pipe ran underground from the safe room to the phone company's lines out at the road, though in fact that telephone had never once been used.

If, however, some phalanx of Che Guevaras actually had launched an attack on Seascape back in those parlous times, Mr. and Mrs. Fritz would simply have locked themselves into the safe room, which included plumbing facilities and stored food, very like a fallout shelter from two decades before, and would have phoned the Palm Beach police to come repel the invaders.

That had never happened, but the room was far from useless. It was impregnable and temperature-controlled, and in it Mrs. Fritz kept her furs, her jewelry, and, in the off-season, much of her best silver. Which meant she never had to join the hoi polloi crowding around the gray mirrors at the bank.

The mirror in the safe room, before which Mrs. Fritz now stood, studying the effect she would make in *this* gown, with *this* necklace, *these* bracelets, *this* brooch, *these* rings, and *this* tiara, was not tinted a discreet gray, like the mirror at the bank. Mrs. Fritz was a realist and didn't need to squint when she gazed upon herself. (Nor would she ever stoop to buy a thirty-year-old husband.) She had lived a long time, and done much, and enjoyed herself thoroughly along the way, and if that life showed its traces on her face and body, what of it? It was an honest life, lived well. She had nothing to hide.

Satisfied with tonight's appearance, Mrs. Fritz left and locked the safe room, then rode the stairlift up to the ground floor, where her walker awaited. Charles LeGrand was her frequent walker, a cultured homosexual probably even older than she was, neat and tidy in his blazer and ascot, smiling from within his very small goatee. Offering his elbow for her hand, "You look *charmante* tonight, Helena," he said.

"Thank you, Charles."

They walked through the ballroom on their way to the car. Mrs. Fritz noted with approval the ranks of rented padded chairs for the bidders, now in rows facing the auctioneer's lectern, each with its numbered paddle waiting on the seat. The platform for the musicians was in place, the side tables were covered in damask but not yet bearing their loads of plates and glasses and cutlery, the portable bar-on-wheels stood ready for tomorrow night's bartender, and all was as it was supposed to be.

The amplifiers under their white tablecloths she didn't even notice.

10

The Voyager's dashboard clock read *7:21* when Leslie steered into the visitors' parking area outside the Elmer Neuman Memorial Hospital in Snake River. Perfect timing.

In her three previous visits to Daniel here, Leslie had learned what she needed to know about the hospital routine. Was this what criminals called "casing the joint"? She knew, for instance, that visiting hours ended at eight P.M., to accommodate visitors who had day jobs. She also knew that down the hall from Daniel lay an old woman named Emily Studworth, who seemed to be permanently unconscious and to never receive visitors. And she further knew that the clerical staff at the hospital changed shift at six P.M.

Leslie shut off the Voyager's engine and looked in the rearview mirror at Loretta. "Okay, Loretta," she said. "We just go and do it and come right back out."

Loretta was already in the wheelchair that Leslie had rented from a place in Riviera Beach called Benson's Sick Room and Party Supplies. Her mulish pouting expression fit the wheelchair very well; she was great in the part.

Leslie got out of the Voyager, slid open its side door, pulled out the ramp, and carefully backed Loretta and the wheelchair down to the blacktop. Then she shut and locked the car, and pushed the wheelchair across the parking lot and up the handicap-access ramp to the hospital's front door.

Since this was the first time she was arriving at the hospital after six P.M., the receptionist who checked the visitors in had never seen her before, and had no way to know that before this she'd always visited a patient named Daniel Parmitt. "Emily Studworth," Leslie told her.

The receptionist nodded and wrote that on her sheet. "You're relatives?"

"We're her grandnieces. Loretta really wanted to see her auntie Emily just once more."

"You don't have much time," the receptionist warned her. "Visiting hours end at eight."

"That's all right, we just want to be with her for a few minutes."

Leslie wheeled Loretta down the hall to the elevators and up to the third floor. The people at the nurses' station gave them a brief incurious look as they came out of the elevator. Leslie smiled at them and pushed the wheelchair down the hall to Daniel's room, which was in semi-darkness, only one small light gleaming yellow on the wall over the bed. They entered, and she pushed the door mostly closed behind her.

He was asleep, but as she entered the room he was suddenly awake, his eyes glinting in the yellow light. She pushed the wheelchair over beside the bed and whispered, "Are you ready?"

"Yes."

"Help me, Loretta."

Obediently, Loretta stood up from the wheelchair and removed the long coat and big-brimmed straw hat. She put them on the bed along with her purse, which had been concealed in the wheelchair. Then she and Leslie helped Daniel get out of bed.

He was stronger each day, but still very weak. The muscles in the sides of his jaw bunched and moved with his determination. He got his legs over the side of the bed, and then, with one of them on either side of him, he made it to his feet.

Leslie said, "Can you stand alone?"

"Yes." It was whispered through gritted teeth.

He stood unmoving, like a tree. They helped him put on the long coat, over the hospital gown that was all he wore, then helped him ease down into the wheelchair. He folded his hands in his lap, to not be noticeable, and Leslie fixed the straw hat on his head.

Meantime, Loretta had sat on the bed to remove

her fake-fur shin-high brown boots. She had soft pumps in her purse that she now slipped on instead.

The boots had been too big for Loretta; they were the right size for Daniel. The hat, the long coat, and the boots covered him completely. As long as he kept his head down and his hands in his lap, he would look exactly like the person Leslie had wheeled in here.

Loretta stood up from the bed, wearing the blue pumps. She had on a shapeless blue-and-white-print dress. "Do I go out now?" she asked.

Leslie considered her. "Don't forget your glasses."

"Oh!" Loretta took her black-framed glasses from her purse and put them on, becoming again the owlish, gawky person Leslie knew.

Leslie said, "You just walk out. We'll be along in a minute."

"All right." Now that they were doing it, and nothing bad was happening, Loretta's mood had improved considerably. She very nearly smiled at Leslie, and when she looked at Daniel in the wheelchair her expression became concerned. "He should stay here," she said.

"He has his reasons," Leslie assured her. "We'll be along."

Loretta left, and Leslie looked in the closet, expecting to find his clothes, surprised to see nothing in there at all. "Where's your things?"

"Cops kept."

"Oh. Well, let's get you out of here."

The return journey was simple, and outside, there was Loretta, waiting for them, standing over there beside the Voyager. As she pushed him across the parking lot, Leslie said, "I don't know what you expect to do tomorrow night."

"Kill some people," he whispered.

11

Jack Young really did care for his new (old) wife, Alice, felt affection for her, enjoyed more about her than her money, though of course the money had come first. In fact, it had been just a joke at the beginning, when he'd met Alice Prester Habib up in New Jersey, where he'd worked for Utica Mutual as a claims examiner, and where, when he first became aware that this particular insured had the hots for him, it was nothing more than the subject of gags around the office.

It was Maureen, an older woman with the firm, computer processor, who'd put the bee in his bonnet. "You could do worse," she'd said, and when Jack thought about it, he *could* do worse, couldn't he? He'd almost *done* worse, two or three times.

It had been almost a year, at that time, since he'd broken up with his last serious girlfriend, or, more accurately, since she'd broken up with him. His life was a little boring, a little same-old same-old, and the idea of shaking it up in this really different and outrageous way came to appeal to him more and more. And don't forget the money.

But the fact is, Alice was okay. God knows she was older than his mother, almost older than his grandmother, but she kept herself in shape like an NFL quarterback, and she was of an age where she had no timidity left in bed at all. So that part wasn't so bad, and for the rest—the knowledge that people laughed at him behind his back, the term "boy toy," which seemed to hover in the air around him like midges— fuck 'em if they couldn't take a joke.

Because you can take the boy out of the actuarial business but you can't take the actuarial business out of the boy, and Jack was fully aware that he was (a) Alice's only heir, attested to in the prenuptial agreement, and (b) likely to outlive her by forty to fifty years. Forty to fifty *rich* years.

So all he had to do was pay attention, in and out of bed, and otherwise be discreet. For instance, when he and Alice walked into the big ballroom at the Breakers Thursday evening for the pre-auction ball, with the tall gleaming mirrors reflecting the posh crowd, and the radiant chandeliers, and the band's swing oldies echoing in the high-ceilinged space, and the swirl of revelers in their sprays of bright colors and gleaming gold and winking silver and sparkling jewels, the very *first* person he saw was Kim Metcalf, and he barely gave her a smile of recognition. She, too, with her shrewd blue eyes under the cloud of fluffy yellow hair, returned only the briefest of impersonal nods, including Alice as much as himself, before she moved on, holding to the arm of her husband, Howard, a retired tax lawyer she'd met as a stew on a first-class flight New York to Chicago. (She was still so much a stew in her heart that to this day she preferred the label "flight attendant.")

As the Metcalfs moved on, Jack turned his eyes firmly away from Kim's twitching creased behind within the shimmering pale blue satin, but his mind said: *Saturday.* The apartment Alice would never know about, down among the condos, where he and Kim managed to meet once or twice every week, came surging into his memory. Kim's body was softer than Alice's, which was also nice, but by now, for the both of them, the main point was to be able to have a conversation with somebody whose memory bank had not become full before you were born.

Turning to Alice and away from all temptation, Jack said, "Do you want to dance, darling, or meet people first?"

"We'll dance, darling," she decided. "We can always meet people."

True enough.

The new red paint on the fire engine doors was dry, and the doors no longer read

CRYSTAL CITY F.D.
ENG #1

Richard Stark

It's a good thing Crystal City, a sparsely populated area down near Homestead, had an Eng #2 as well, or the good folks there would be shit out of luck if a fire were to start up anywhere around town in the next couple of days. It was a volunteer fire department, like so many in the sticks, so there was never anybody around the small brick fire house except for fires and meetings, so it had been very easy, at five this morning, to bypass the alarm system and ease into the fire house and come roaring out with old Eng #1. By the time anybody started looking for it, Melander and Carlson and Ross would have finished with it.

At nine P.M., with the pre-auction ball in full swing up at the Breakers, Ross stood beside the driver's door of Eng #1, an open quart of gold enamel paint in his left hand and an M. Grumbacher fine-line brush #5 in his right, with Melander just behind him to hold the flashlight. The fire engine now stood on the lawn at the right side of the house, out of sight from anywhere off the property. Ross, who had learned to be a passable sign painter during the first of his two stretches inside, leaned close to the door and drew the first vertical, then the U-shape to the right:

P

Farley's wife had learned to sleep through the late-night phone calls, and Farley had trained himself to wake right up at the beginning of the first ring, his hand snaking out from under the covers toward the phone before his eyes had completely focused on the bedside clock: *1:14.* There'd been worse.

"Farley."

"Higgins here, Sarge," being one of the deputies on night shift at the office. "We got a report of a missing man out to the hospital."

"Parmitt," Farley said.

"That's right, Daniel Parmitt. The night administrator just called. They did their usual late-night check on the patients, and that one's gone."

How? He didn't walk out, Parmitt, he wasn't up to it. Somebody helped him. The real estate woman? Farley said, "You sent somebody over there?"

"Jackson and Reese."

"Call them, tell them I'm on my way." There wouldn't be anything there; still, he'd have a look.

Damn; should've taken those prints yesterday.

He drove into Snake River at two in the morning in the rented Buick Regal. He'd be done here in an hour, then drive back to Miami International, have breakfast, take the morning flight west, be swimming in his own pool by midafternoon.

The woman who gave him his assignments, once or twice a year, was a lawyer in Chicago. They spoke guardedly on the phone, almost never met face-to-face, and unless he was on assignment he lived a quiet life indeed, writing occasional album reviews for music magazines. On assignment, he had a different name, different identification, different credit card, different everything. Different personality. He didn't even listen to music, driving south and west from Miami.

The lawyer in Chicago had told him this wasn't a rush job, but what was the point in dragging it out? Fly in, do it, fly away. "Just so it's certain," the lawyer had said, and he had said, "It's certain," because when you hired him, you hired the best. It had been certain every single time for the last twelve years.

Apparently, the client, whoever he was, had gone bargain basement the first time, brought in people who'd messed the job up, left the target alive but hospitalized. And the client really and positively wanted this target worse than sick; he wanted this target a fading memory.

He had never before had a target stationary in a hospital. And no guards on him round the clock, no steady police presence. It was almost too easy, as though he shouldn't take his full fee for the job. Though he would. Still, it hardly seemed like work for a grown man, and he had to talk to himself as he parked the Regal on a side street three blocks from the hospital to walk the rest of the way. He had to remind himself that *all* assignments are serious, even if this one seemed like shooting ducks in a rain barrel. He had to remind himself that every mistake was serious and that overconfidence is the cause of more mistakes than anything else. He had to remind himself to treat this assignment just as though there might be some danger in it.

He approached the hospital catty-corner, through

the parking lots. He was a tall lean man dressed all in black. One Beretta was in a holster in the small of his back, just above the belt, and the other was in his left boot. The right boot contained the throwing knife. Other than that, and his knowledge of several martial arts, he was unarmed; he never carried more weaponry than needed when on assignment.

The hospital's main entrance and the emergency entrance around on the left side were both well lit, but the service entrance on the right was dark except for one small illuminated globe mounted on the wall above the door. He found the door unlocked—he'd have picked it if necessary—went in, and climbed one flight of concrete stairs before stepping through into a hallway. What he needed first was an operating room.

He avoided the lit-up nurse's stations, moved through the halls, and soon found what he was looking for. And in the scrub-up room next door were several clean sets of green O.R. coats and pants. He took the largest set and put them on over his clothing; then he'd be able to move more freely along the halls, though still keeping out of other people's way.

There had been no way to find out ahead of time what room the target was in, so all he could do was walk the halls and look at the patient names stuck into the labels outside the doors. How long could it take? Half an hour?

Less. Fifteen minutes after he entered the hospital, he came to the third-floor door labeled "Parmitt," and without breaking stride or looking around he walked right in. Never pause and look indecisive, it attracts attention.

The target should be asleep; the knife would probably do. He crossed the dim room to the bed, starting to reach down toward his right boot, then realized the bed was empty.

Bathroom? Not away to therapy or anything like that, not at this hour. He looked around, saw the closed bathroom door, and walked around the bed.

He was almost to the bathroom when someone entered the room behind him, saying, "Doctor, we'd rather nobody touched anything in—what the hell, we can turn the light on."

He spun around as the overhead fluorescents flickered on, and saw the rangy man in tan sheriff's uniform in the doorway, and thought, I can be a doctor. Thirty seconds and I'm out of here.

"Whatever you say, Sheriff," he said with an easy smile, and started toward the door.

But the sheriff was suddenly frowning. "What's that under your scrubs?"

He wasn't prepared for in-close observation. "Just my shirt, Sheriff," he said, already stooping toward the boot with the Beretta in it, as he casually talked on, saying, "I get chilly at night."

"Stop," the sheriff said, and all at once had his side arm out and aimed, in the classic two-handed bent-kneed stance. "Straighten up with your hands empty," he said.

He didn't dare bend any more, but he didn't

straighten either. "Sheriff? What the heck are you doing?"

"I always hit what I aim at," the sheriff told him. "And with you, what I'll aim at is your knee." Then he raised his voice, shouting toward the doorway behind him: "Reese! Jackson!"

He heard the rumble of running footsteps as he said, "Sheriff? I don't know what your problem—"

Two uniformed deputies appeared in the doorway, trying not to look excited, one of them black, the other one white. The black, staring, said, "Sarge? Who's *this?*"

"Exhibit one," the sheriff said. His hands holding that automatic were as solid as a rock. "You two search him, see what armament he's got on him."

He thought: Can I go through the window? Thick plate glass, I'd either bounce off or get cut to pieces on the way out. Third floor. Three of them; what to do?

The deputies approached him, keeping out of their sergeant's line of fire. The sergeant said, "If it happens you do have to shoot the son of a bitch, take out his legs. *This* one we're gonna keep alive."

12

After lunch, Leslie went shopping for Daniel, using the list he'd given her of his sizes. He had nothing, so she bought two sets of everything from the skin out, plus one pair of black loafers, and a small canvas bag to put it all in. It stretched her credit card, but he had given her a bank to call in San Antonio and a PIN, and the man there had confirmed that ten thousand dollars would be shifted to the real estate agency's escrow account by noon tomorrow, where she'd be able to withdraw it without trouble.

Be nice to have a banker in San Antonio who'd wire you ten thousand dollars whenever you felt like it. Be nice to understand Daniel Parmitt, too, but she doubted she ever would.

Done shopping and with the canvas bag in the trunk of her car, she next showed seven condos to a couple from Branson, Missouri, who didn't like any of them, and when she got back to the office Sergeant Farley was there, the sheriff from Snake River.

She'd been expecting this, she having been Daniel's only visitor in the hospital, but it still frightened her when she saw the man standing beside her desk in his crisp tan uniform. It made her tense up, suddenly unsure of her ability to deceive him.

"Why, Sergeant," she said, smiling, coming boldly forward, "what brings you here?" Then, affecting sudden concern to hide her nervousness, she said, "Has something happened? Is Daniel all right?"

"Something happened, okay," he said, and gestured at the client chair beside her desk. "Okay if we sit for a minute?"

"Of course. Do."

She was aware of the other reps throwing little surreptitious glances in this direction, but they were the least of her worries. She'd intended to bring Daniel his new clothes after writing up this afternoon's wasted work, but did she dare, with Sergeant Farley around?

They sat turned toward one another, and he said, "To come right out with it, Parmitt's gone."

She acted as though she didn't understand. "Gone? You don't mean—no. I don't know what you mean."

"He left the hospital last night," Farley said.

"But how could he? He's so weak."

"We figure," Farley said, "somebody gave him some help. I was wondering, would that be you?"

"Me?" Don't overplay this, she told herself. "He never *asked* me," she said, then frowned at the papers on her desk as she said, "I don't even think I would. He shouldn't be out of the hospital, he's too sick." Then she looked at Farley again, saw him coolly watching her, and said, "He shouldn't *be* anywhere else. Are you looking for him?"

"Checked all the motels round about," he told her. "Talked to the cabbies, checked the bus terminal. Got no cars stolen. You're right, Parmitt didn't go out of there on his own, he had help."

"Well, it wasn't me," she said. "Last night, was it?"

"Sometime before one. Between eight and one, we figure."

"I was home," she said, "with my mother and my sister, watching TV. I don't know if your own family is considered a good alibi, but that's where I was."

"Okay," he said, then seemed to think things over for a minute. "The point is," he said, "anybody around Parmitt is likely to be in trouble."

"For helping him, you mean."

"No, a different kind of trouble. We caught a fella in the hospital last night, came there to kill our Mr. Parmitt."

That did astonish her. "My God! No!"

"Yes. Might of slipped in and out, nobody the wiser, except we were already on the scene, account of Parmitt being gone. So now we got this fella, and pretty soon he'll tell us who hired him, and then we'll learn a lot more about Daniel Parmitt than we know right now."

"Good," she said.

"But the thing is," Farley told her, "this is the second try at him we know about, the first being the gunshot put him in the hospital. Before we catch up with the fella that's paying for all this, some other goon might catch up with Parmitt. And probably anybody standing too close to him."

"Thank you, Sergeant," she said. "I understand what you're saying. Just in case I *am* involved with Daniel, I should know to watch out. But I'm not." The laugh she offered was almost completely real. "Speeding tickets is as big a criminal as I've ever been."

"Good, keep it that way," he said, and got to his feet, at last. She also rose, as he said, "If you hear from him, I'd appreciate a call."

"Absolutely," she said. "And if *you* find out anything about him, would you let me know?"

"Will do." He extended a hand. "Nice to meet you, Ms. Mackenzie."

He's got a thing for me, she thought, as they shook hands, but he'd never show it in a million years. She said, "I guess I can cross Daniel Parmitt off my list of eligible bachelors."

His grin was just a little sour. "Good idea," he said.

She had Daniel stashed in the condo where he'd first told her about the three men who planned to rob tonight's jewelry auction. That condo had now been sold, by her, but the closing hadn't happened yet, so nobody would have any reason to go in there for a couple of weeks. She'd brought him in last night, with the help of Loretta, who was suddenly happy and perky and full of good cheer now that the scary part was over, and they'd left him with milk and candy bars and two blankets.

Now, once she was sure Farley wasn't still around and following her, she drove back down to the condo, carried the canvas bag in with her, and found Parker seated on the bench on the terrace, where they'd talked the first time. He had one of the blankets wrapped around himself.

"I have clothes for you," she said, and showed him the canvas bag.

He got up stiffly, but he could move better today than last night. He took the bag from her and went off to another room, and when he came back, dressed, he looked almost his normal self, but more gaunt, and still moving slowly. "I could use a razor," he said as he sat on the terrace bench again. His voice at last was above a whisper, was now a hoarse burr, like a palm brushing corduroy.

She sat beside him, saying, "Okay. Anything else?"

"Can you pick me up at seven-thirty?"

"Daniel, you still want to go after those people? Tonight?"

"Tonight's when they're doing it."

"But you're—I don't suppose I could argue you out of it."

"If you argue me out of it," he said, "you don't get anything."

"If they kill you I don't get anything either."

"Maybe it won't happen."

"Maybe," she said, giving up. "Sergeant Farley came to see me this afternoon."

He watched her. "Did he worry you?"

"A little," she admitted. "But he had more news."

"What?"

She told him about the hired killer Farley had captured. He grunted at that and said, "That's the end of it, then."

"But who is he? Who's after you like this?"

"The stupid thing is," he said, "I don't know. The guy's making trouble, and he doesn't have to."

"I don't understand."

"I got some identification from a guy," he said.

"Daniel Parmitt's identification?"

He shrugged. "He's a guy who does that kind of thing. He did it for somebody else, South American or Central American I think, maybe a drug guy or a general, whoever. Turns out that guy wants to erase anybody knows about his changeover. He sent people to kill the guy did the work for him. I was there, he thinks I know his story, too, he's tracking me down. Only now the law's gonna follow the string back from the guy they just nabbed, and they're gonna find him, and his cover's blown. He must be wanted badly somewhere, and it'll come out. You'll read about it in the papers, a month or two from now, some guy everybody's after, he suddenly pops up."

"But you're not concerned about him," she said. "He tries to kill you, and it doesn't matter to you.

These other people, you feel they cheated you, that's all, but you won't give up."

"The other guy's gonna self-destruct," he told her. "He has to, he's too stupid to last. He's somebody used to power, not brains. But these three are mechanics, we had an understanding, they broke it. They don't do that." He shrugged. "It makes sense, or it doesn't."

Did anything about Daniel Parmitt make sense? Getting to her feet, she said, "I'll see you at seven-thirty. With the razor."

13

At seven, the big doors were opened onto the driveway to Mrs. Fritz's house, and the police car drove in to park just off the gravel, facing out. The private security people set up their lectern on the left side of the entrance and stood around waiting, but no one was going to be unfashionably on time, and the first guests didn't arrive till seven-twelve.

Each car stopped at the lectern, where the driver handed over to the guard the invitation the guest had received last night after making his sealed bid on one of the items up for auction. The guard checked the invitation against the list on his lectern, then politely nodded the guest through. At the main entrance, staff opened the car doors, the partygoers emerged, the driver was given a claim check, and the car was driven by a valet around to the parking area at the side.

*   *   *

Just over half a mile to the south, Melander and Carlson and Ross had started to dress. Stacked on the dining room table and on the floor were their fire boots, their rubberized gloves, red fire helmets, and black turnout coats with the reflective horizontal yellow stripes and, in block yellow letters on the back, PBFD. Leaning against a wall were their three black air canisters, also with PBFD on them in block white letters. When completely dressed, their visored eye-guards and the mouthpieces from their air canisters would cover their faces entirely.

"I love a costume party," Ross said.

A few miles farther south, Leslie stood in the bathroom doorway and watched Daniel shave off that ridiculous little mustache. It changed him. Without the mustache, he was a hard man, very cold. She realized with surprise that, if she'd seen him this way at first, she wouldn't have dared approach him.

He was still battered, though, and she didn't see how he could hope to beat those three men. He'd stripped to the waist to shave, and his torso was still swathed in bandages, partly because of the bullet holes front and back but mostly because of the broken ribs. Why wouldn't they just ride right over him?

And what happens to me? she wondered.

Mrs. Fritz's ballroom quickly filled. All the men wore essentially what they'd worn at the Breakers last night, and all the women wore something strikingly different. Staff moved among them with canapés and champagne, and special lights gleamed on the display tables where the jewelry was arrayed. Maroon velvet ropes kept the guests from getting within reaching distance of the jewelry. Everybody was here now except the musicians, who would arrive later, and play for dancing after the auction was complete. To one side, Mrs. Fritz and the auctioneer, a professional man who'd worked any number of charity balls around here over the years, consulted together about timing.

"I think it's time," Melander said, and the three of them, encumbered in their full firefighter gear, tromped out of the house and around to the fire engine parked at the side. Carlson climbed up behind the wheel while Melander and Ross took up standing positions on the outside of the fire engine, just to increase the visual plausibility of the thing.

Carlson said, "Ready?" and the other two agreed they were ready. Carlson picked up the two small radio transmitters from the seat beside him and pressed down on the buttons.

In the ballroom, the incendiary rockets came thundering out of the amplifiers still in the corner. Some of the rockets flew straight up, to embed themselves in the ceiling and spray sparks and flame onto the people below. Some shot directly back into the wall, gouting flame and smoke, and the rest drilled down into the floor. None were aimed at the guests or the display tables of jewelry.

Shocking heat and noise and smoke abruptly filled the room. No one knew what had happened, where this sudden disaster had come from. A lot of people thought rockets were being fired from outside the house. Everybody milled around in sudden fear, trying to find a way out. The display tables and the auctioneer's stand blocked the terrace doors, so the only way out was through the broad interior doorway into the rest of the house. People jammed together, making a bottleneck in the doorway, clawing to get through.

Outside, the police and the security guards stared in amazement at the sudden fire burning on the roof, listened unbelievingly to the screams from inside the house, gaped at each other in bewilderment, not knowing what they were supposed to do. Then, almost immediately it seemed, they felt the great relief of hearing that approaching siren.

The fire engine came rushing up from the south, red lights flashing, siren yowling. Police and guards cleared everybody out of the entranceway, and the fire engine went tearing around the curve, Melander and Ross clinging to the handholds, the fire engine rushing full tilt at the house, where the first of the fleeing guests were just now beginning to stagger out into the clear night air.

Carlson didn't hit the brake until the very last second, the big fire engine spewing gravel as it shuddered to a stop. He switched off the motor and took the key with him, to cause a little extra trouble down the line, but left the siren on, screaming away, so communication among the other people present would be just that much more difficult.

Leslie helped Daniel into his shirt, and the two of them gathered up everything that had been brought into the condo. She said, "Are you sure, Daniel?"

"Time to go," he said.

The three firemen ran heavy-footed through the house, pushing the panicked guests out of their way, finally helping the last of the guests and staff out of the ballroom. They slammed the double doors and slid a massive sideboard over the polished floor and up against the doors to block them.

Alice Prester Young staggered out of the house alone, into the glare and scream of the big fire engine, with more fire engines coming now from far away, racing south. She'd lost Jack somewhere, she'd been terrified, she had to struggle through the awful crowd completely on her own.

Where was Jack? Was he hurt, crushed by the people back there? Where was Jack?

She stared around at the people collapsing on the lawn, and all at once she saw Jack, and he was *carrying* somebody, in his arms, like a groom carrying a bride. He was reeling like a drunken man, but he was carrying a woman, and as he at last put her on her

feet on the lawn Alice saw she was young Kim Metcalf, Howard Metcalf's sexpot stewardess wife. And as
she saw them, Jack saw her and stopped dead.

The stupid thing is, she hadn't thought anything
until Jack stopped like that, like . . . like a caught burglar. And Kim's look of shock and guilt when she
met Alice's eyes across the reeling, weeping, stunned
crowd, there was that, too.

Movement to her left. Alice turned her suddenly
heavy head, and Howard Metcalf stood there, near
her on the steps, gazing out and down at his wife.
With great difficulty, Alice turned her heavy head
again and looked at Jack, and now he seemed to have
no expression on his face at all, like a bad drawing, or
a minor figure in the background of a comic strip.

In all that racket, there was a great silence, enclos-
ing the four of them.

In the ballroom, Melander and Carlson and Ross
quickly shimmied out of their gloves, helmets, air
tanks, fire boots, and turnout coats. Beneath, they
each wore a black wet suit and a large zippered bag
on a belt around the waist. The bags now held nothing but divers' face masks and headlamps, which they
removed so they could load the bags with all of
Miriam Hope Clendon's jewelry.

Leslie and Daniel drove northward in her Lexus,
neither saying anything, he resting his head back,
eyes closed. Conserving himself. Then he opened his
eyes and looked out ahead and said, "Slow down."

She did, but said, "Why?"

Instead of answering, he opened his window. She had the air-conditioning on, of course, and now the humid air billowed in, and with it a faint distant sound of sirens. She said, "Police?"

He laughed, a sound like a bark. "Fire engine," he said. "I told you they were gaudy. They aren't going in from the sea after all, they're going in from the land, in a fire engine."

"But there isn't any fire," she said.

"With them? There's a fire. It's along here now."

He meant Mr. Roderick's house, or whoever Mr. Roderick really was. As he closed his window, she said, "Do you want me to come in with you?"

"No. You go home. I'll call you tomorrow."

"What if you don't?"

"Then I don't," he said. "Stop here."

She rolled to a stop near the Roderick house, and he paused, his hand on the door handle. "The question is, how do they get back out? Tuxes under the fire coats?"

She said, "To mingle with the guests, you mean? Could they do that?"

"They think they can do anything," he said, and opened the door. "I'll call you tomorrow."

At the Fritz house, more fire engines had arrived, blocked by the milling crowd and the still-screaming first fire engine that none of the later firefighters recognized. "Whose is this? Is this from West Palm? What the hell's it doing here?"

In the ballroom, Melander and Carlson and Ross finished loading the jewelry into their waist bags. They put the air canisters back on, put on the divers' face masks and the mouthpieces and the headlamps. From hooks inside their turnout coats they brought out pairs of black flippers.

Leslie found a place to park, locked the Lexus, and walked back down the road toward Mr. Roderick's house.

Firemen hurried through the mansion and found the ballroom doors wedged shut. They had their axes and used them, splintering the doors.

Melander and Carlson and Ross heard the thuds of the axes. Melander shoved a display case out of the way and they went through the terrace doors and ran across the terrace, invisible in their black wet suits, holding their flippers in their hands. A little apart from one another, so they wouldn't collide underwater, they dove into the sea.

Firemen smashed their way into the ballroom. Police followed. As the rockets fizzled out and the fires began to fade, they looked around at the emptiness.

All gone.

FOUR

1

If he didn't exert himself, the pains in his chest were just a small irritation, a low grumbling, like far-off thunder. But when he had to move, even to do simple things like pull on pants, the pain punched him all over again, like brand-new, like the bullet thudding into him right now instead of a week ago. Still, he didn't mind the pain as much as the weakness, especially in his legs. He wasn't used to being dialed down like this; he kept expecting the strength, and it wasn't there.

The worst part of getting into the house was the climb over the windowsill. He found the suction-cup handles where he'd left them, attached them to the pane of glass he'd scored, removed the glass, and reached in to unlock and open the window. Then he put the glass pane through the opening and stretched to rest it on the floor inside, leaning against the wall.

That was the first punch. His breathing was constricted anyway, because of the bandages around his ribs, and the punch constricted it even more, so that he inhaled with hoarse sounds that he'd have to control later, in the house.

He hoisted himself over the windowsill, gritting his teeth, not blacking out, but lying on his back on the floor until the pain receded and his breath was closer to normal. Then he stood, shut the window, dropped the suction-cup handles through the open pane into the shrubbery outside, and fitted the piece of glass back into place.

He had time to search the house, but not long. There were two changes in the garage: the white Bronco was there, the same one they'd used after the bank robbery, and the trunk where he'd found their weapons was open and empty. Did they have the guns with them, on the job?

No. All six were on the dining room table, the three automatics and the three shotguns. The Sentinel was still under the table. He left it there; what he needed to do would be done differently.

In the living room, the alarm system had been switched on. Its warning light gleamed red, though Parker had seen to it that it would not respond to break-ins. And in the kitchen, the refrigerator was now full of food, as were the shelves. So they planned to spend a few days here, until things calmed down, which was smart.

Parker made his way through the house, slowly, noting the changes, pausing to lean against a wall when the weakness got to be too much. He came last to the big empty room with the piano in the corner and the glass wall facing the sea, and out there lights now moved back and forth, police boats with searchlights, roving this way and that, like dogs who've lost a scent. So the trio had gone to the robbery by land, in a fire engine or some other official vehicle, but they'd left by sea.

Soon they'd be back here. In a boat? Or were they diving? Probably diving.

He didn't have much time to find a hiding place. He had to be secure, but somewhere that would make it possible to move around. He went up to the second floor, tried all the shut doors up there, and found a staircase leading up to the attic. It was covered with black industrial carpet and didn't make a sound.

The attic area at the top of the stairs had been converted into a screening room, probably by the movie star couple, and then later all the projection equipment had been taken out again, leaving two dozen plush swivel chairs facing a screen attached to the wall. The screening room had been meant to look like a thirties movie house, with art deco lighting sconces and dark red fabric on the walls. There was no reason for the three to come up here, so this was where Parker would wait until he could get at them.

He went back down to the second floor and out one of the bedrooms to the upstairs terrace. Lights

229

still moved back and forth in the thick darkness, but Parker knew the police boats were searching too far out, probably expecting to find a boat. But the three would stick close to shore as they made their way back, without a boat.

He sat on one of the chaises, feet up, and watched the lights roam out there. So long as they stayed out there, restlessly moving, Melander and Carlson and Ross had not been caught. So they had a good operation, and they were now on their way to Parker with twelve million dollars in jewelry.

It was good to sit here for a minute, after the exertion of moving through the house, but he didn't want to get too comfortable and fall asleep. He could sleep later.

The dim flashlight had been moving on the beach for a minute or two before his mind told him what his eyes were looking at. A small light, fainter and more diffuse than the searchlights out over the ocean, was headed this way up the beach from the water. The three, coming back?

One of them. And it wasn't a flashlight, it was a headlamp. The figure beneath it was black, almost impossible to see as he came forward across the sand. Parker lost sight of the lamp and the hurrying man as he neared the retaining wall at the edge of the property, then he heard the loud rusty squeal as the gate at the foot of the narrow concrete stairs was opened.

Here came the headlamp, up the stairs to the terrace. And beyond him, two more lights were now coming from the sea.

All three of them. Parker got to his feet and stood back by the door, ready to go inside.

The first one down below stopped on the terrace and was taking something bulky off his back. A scuba tank. And now the other two came up, also removing scuba tanks, and the first one spoke, and it was Melander: "Did you see the dolphin?"

"No. What dolphin?" That was Carlson, the driver.

"He crossed right in front of us."

"You were out ahead, you were making some sort of race out of it."

"I wanted to get back."

Ross, the third one, said, "In the morning, early, we gotta sweep the sand down there."

Carlson said, "Why?"

"You see those lights? They'll stay out there till daylight, and when they're sure we didn't get picked up in a boat they'll come back in and search the island, and one thing they'll look for is footprints coming in from the sea."

Melander said, "Jerry, you're right. I never would have thought of that, and tomorrow morning they'd be all over my ass."

Carlson said, "First light, the cops'll be out, too, maybe they see us sweeping. We should do it now."

Melander said, "Let me get out of this wet suit, and then I'll do anything you want."

They started to move toward the house, carrying their scuba tanks. They were almost out of sight from

Parker's vantage point, and he was about to step inside, when everybody heard the sudden squeak of the gate down below, abruptly stopped.

Melander was fast. He didn't bother with the stairs, just ran forward, vaulted over the railing, and dropped the seven feet to the sand below.

Parker heard the woman cry out in sudden fear, and knew immediately it was Leslie. Wanting to be sure she got hers, wanting to hang around and observe from just out of sight, and immediately got herself caught.

Ross and Carlson ran down the stairs to take a hand. Would they kill her? That would be the simplest, for Parker and for them both, kill her and throw the body in the ocean and forget about it.

No. They were bringing her up the stairs. They were curious, they wanted to ask her some questions, complicate things a little more.

Parker watched the three dark men come up, headlamps bobbing, the paler figure of Leslie struggling in their midst. She was protesting, stupid half-sentences, pretending to be just an innocent bystander, nothing to do with anything, which they would not buy for a minute. They've just come back from the biggest heist in Palm Beach history, and here's a woman trying to sneak into their house. Not a coincidence.

But Parker didn't expect the conclusion that Melander leaped to, as easily as he'd leaped over the wall. While Leslie continued to struggle and to argue, Melander shook her with the one hand holding her arm and said, "Don't make me punch you, okay? You gotta shut up now so we can talk."

She did shut up then, shrinking into herself as she looked at the three of them, looming over her, encased in black, with the headlamps shining in her eyes. Parker saw her face unnaturally white against the darkness all around as she forced herself to be silent.

And Melander had a touch of gloating humor in his voice when he said, "Claire Willis, am I right? We visited your house, up north, sorry you weren't there."

She blinked at them, baffled. "What?"

Melander said, "So that means our friend Parker's around someplace, too. He'd probably like us to take good care of you, right? Let's go inside. You could be valuable to us."

Damn. Almost as irritated with Leslie as with the other three, Parker faded into the house and up the attic stairs. Leslie didn't have a purse with her, and probably didn't have ID, and wouldn't be able to prove who she was. So let them thrash it out together all they wanted. Sooner or later, they'd go to sleep.

2

But he went to sleep first, not intending to, and woke when the wall sconce lights came on, then heard them coming up the stairs. Why? To have a place to keep their prisoner.

When he'd first come up, in the darkness, he'd sat on one of the swivel chairs with his feet on another, but the curved position was bad for his ribs, bad all around, and he gave up and lay on his back on the black-carpeted floor. He didn't think he'd sleep, it wasn't that late. Melander and Carlson and Ross had done the robbery a little after eight, just barely night, then full night by the time they got back to this house, after eight-thirty. They'd be keyed up, and now they'd have Leslie to distract them, so they wouldn't go to sleep until late. Parker figured he shouldn't go downstairs until at least three in the morning, so he had six hours up here to rest.

But he hadn't expected to sleep. Normally, he could hold sleep off until the work at hand was done, but this was some other part of the weakness. He'd been awake, lying on his back in the darkness among all the swivel chairs, planning how he would take them out, and now he was awake again, the red-tinged lights clicking on, the swivel chairs like flying saucers above him.

He heard them coming up the stairs, Melander saying, "This is a nice quiet place for you till the morning, keep you out of trouble."

Parker rolled against the wall farthest from the stairs, black clothing against black carpet, turned away so the paleness of his face and hands wouldn't show.

"What is this?" That was Leslie, still trying to catch up.

Melander, the grin in his voice, said, "The previous owners used to watch their own movies in here. Think how much fun people used to have in this room. Maybe if you're real quiet, you can hear the singing and the dancing and the laughing."

"And if you're not real quiet," Carlson said, "you'll hear from us."

"Oh, come on, Hal," Melander said. "Claire's gonna cooperate, aren't you, Claire?"

"I've told you I'm not—"

Slap. Melander's voice, no longer humorous: "And *I've* told *you,* quit insulting my intelligence. I'm losing my good disposition, Claire, you follow me?"

235

Silence from Leslie. Ross said, "She'll be all right now, Boyd. Won't you?"

"Please . . ."

"See?" Now Ross was being the good cop, saying, "Here's the light switch here, you can turn it on or off, whatever you want. The door's gonna be locked down there, but we'll let you out in the morning, we'll have a good breakfast, talk it over."

"That's right," Melander said, in a good mood again. "No more excitement for tonight. You go on over there and sit down. Go on, now, just go right over by those chairs and—"

Her *shriek* at that second was not because they'd hit her again or anything like that. Parker knew exactly what it was. Coming deeper into the room, she'd piped him, and immediately tipped him to the others, like a bird dog.

She'd been better than the normal amateur, until it mattered.

Yes. Here came the footsteps and Melander's humorous surprise, saying, "And what have we here?"

Parker rolled over onto his back to look up at them. Carlson and Ross carried the automatics he'd ruined. He said, "You boys pulled a nice one today," hating the reediness of his voice.

Carlson said, "And you thought you'd wait till we were asleep and take it away from us."

"Just keeping an eye on my share," Parker said.

Melander said, "On your feet."

"He's been *shot!*" Leslie blurted. "He isn't even supposed to be out of the hospital!"

They frowned at her, and then down at Parker. Melander said, "Is that right?"

"Shot in the chest," Parker said. "Some broken ribs. I'll live."

"Maybe," Carlson said.

Melander backed away a pace. "Okay, Parker," he said. "You can stay up here with—"

Leslie said, "*That's* Parker?"

Before Melander could smack her again, Parker said, "Give it up, Claire, we folded that hand."

She blinked at him, but at last she was beginning to get her wits about her, and she didn't argue the point.

Ross came forward, saying, "You bandaged and stuff?"

"Around the chest."

"Where you carrying? I'll just ease it out without making trouble for you."

Parker shook his head. "Not carrying. I don't want you to think I'm still sore."

They didn't believe him. Melander, laughing, said, "We come in peace? Check him out, Jerry."

Ross handed his automatic to Carlson and went to one knee beside Parker. "Sorry about this," he said.

"Go ahead."

Ross patted him down without unnecessary pain, then shrugged and looked up at the other two. "He's clean."

"Will wonders never cease," Melander said. "Okay, Parker, we'll talk in the morning. Your investment came through, right?"

"Right," Parker said.

Ross took his dead automatic back from Carlson, and the three of them went downstairs, murmuring together, a little confused. Parker was here, but hurt, and unarmed. What did it mean?

The lock clicked on the door downstairs. Leslie said, "I'm sorry, Daniel. It's all my fault."

"Yes," he said.

3

He sat on the floor, back against the wall. The hard surfaces were best, when he was awake. She sat in one of the swivel chairs. She said, "You were going to hide up here until they were asleep and then go down and kill them, weren't you?"

"Yes."

"How?"

"Pillow for Carlson and Ross. Melander last, the big one, with a bullet. They're in separate rooms."

"Are you strong enough to do that? With the pillow?"

"I'm not going to find out," he said.

"Because of me."

"Yes."

"If you weren't strong enough, you'd use a knife?"

"No. You can't do a real job with a knife and stay clean. There's tools in the kitchen. Hammers."

"Oh." She blinked, and licked her lips, and moved on away from that, saying, "If it wasn't for me, they wouldn't have had any reason to come up here, and they wouldn't have found you."

"That's right."

"But why tell them I'm Claire? Is Claire your girl-friend?"

"If they think you're Claire," Parker said, "they'll think I want to keep you alive, so you're a bargaining chip in their favor. Keeps them calm."

"But you don't care if I live or die," she said, "do you?"

"I'd rather you were dead," he said.

She thought about that. "Are you going to kill me?"

"No."

"Because of the bargaining chip."

"Yes."

"You're a little more truthful than I'm ready for," she said.

He shrugged.

She said, "Is there a bathroom up here?"

He pointed at the door in the rear wall, to the left of the stairs. "No window, it's vented."

"I wasn't planning to call for help or anything," she said, and got to her feet and went away to the bathroom.

While she was gone, he thought it over. Should he wait until later, then try to get down through that door at the foot of the stairs? No; they knew he was here, and they didn't trust him, and they'd have the door covered with all kinds of traps, things to make noise, alarms going off. On the other hand, every hour that he kept still his body improved a little more. In the morning, he'd be better able to deal with them.

But the original plan was dead. And Leslie, who'd been a help before this, was now no help at all. Now she was trouble.

She came back out of the bathroom and came over to sit in a chair near him. She looked very solemn, as though she'd made an oath of some kind in the bathroom. She said, "I've never been around anything like this before."

"I know that."

"The idea of killing somebody, that doesn't bother you."

He waited.

"It does bother me," she said, "but that's all right. I got us into a hard place, and I know I did. I don't think they'll just let me go."

"No."

"I think tomorrow," she said, "they'll decide to kill us both, once they've talked it over together."

"Probably."

"If it was just me, I wouldn't have a chance. If it was just you, without me, I think you would stand a chance."

"Maybe."

"I don't want to get in the way anymore," she said. "Whatever you say to do, I'll do. If it's just sit down and shut up, I'll sit down and shut up. If I can do anything to help, I'll do it."

He said, "That way, through that other door there, is the unfinished part of the attic. I didn't get a chance to look it over. I want to know about windows, and I want something soft between me and the floor, so I can sleep without getting too stiff."

"I'll be right back," she said, and was gone almost ten minutes, and came back dragging a large gray canvas painters' tarpaulin. "Small windows, with bars," she said. "Decorative bars, but bars. There's this, and there's part of a roll of pink insulation. I thought we could put the insulation on the floor and part of the tarp on top of it, and put the rest of the tarp over us."

"Good," he said.

While she was gone this time, he went on all fours to the nearest chair and climbed it to his feet. The few hours of sleep had stiffened him, more than he liked to think about. He didn't have *time* for the body to heal; it had to come along no matter what.

She came in with the roll of insulation, pulling it along, and they worked together to put down four strips of it, pink side down, shiny paper side up. Then they stretched the middle section of the tarp over it, with extra material on both sides to pull over them.

She said, "Do you want the light on or off?"

"I'm going to sleep," he said.

The laugh she gave had hysteria in it. "Are you kidding? In the spot we're in, and in the condition you're in, who's going to do anything *except* sleep? I'll turn off the light."

4

She said, "What's Claire like?"

"No, Leslie."

But she was following her own line of thought, answering her own question. "I think she's very beautiful and very self-sufficient. Neither of you leans on the other, you both stand up straight."

"Sure," he said.

She considered him. "I need somebody . . . a little different," she decided.

He shook his head. "You don't need anybody, Leslie."

She surprised him by blushing. She turned away, then turned back and smiled sheepishly and said, "I'd like to need somebody. I keep thinking, if I find the right guy, I'll need him."

"Could be."

"That's how it is with you and Claire, I suppose."

He knew this talk was simply so she could distract herself from the people downstairs. Her watch had told them it was almost eight-thirty in the morning, so whatever was going to happen would happen soon. But he didn't feel like playing the game anymore, so he walked around instead, in and among the swivel chairs, rolling his shoulders, judging how his body felt this morning.

A little better, maybe, just a little better. His voice seemed stronger to him, and the night on the fairly hard flat surface—the insulation hadn't done much—seemed to have been good for his ribs.

She sat in a swivel chair, swiveling slowly back and forth, watching him move. They were both silent for a few minutes, and then she said, "I'm hungry."

"So am I."

"Should we knock on the door or something?"

"Let them have their own pace."

"Okay." Then, in a rush: "Are they going to kill us?"

"I don't know," he said, and stood still, hand on the back of one of the chairs. Now that she was ready, they could talk. He said, "Melander's the main guy, the big one with all the hair, and as far as he's concerned they were all reasonable back when. He just borrowed money from me, and he meant to pay me back, and he might even pay me back someday. He thinks he's straight in our world, that he doesn't heist a heister, and what happened with me was just business or something."

She said, "Could you let it *be* just business or something?"

"We'll see how it plays out," he said, to keep her calm. "There's Carlson, I think he'd prefer we were dead. He doesn't like it that I didn't wait at home like a good boy, that I'm here."

"And the other one?"

"Ross follows. He'll follow whoever's on top."

She thought about all that, slowly shaking her head. Her right shoe was half off, and she waggled it up and down with her toes. Then she said, "What do you think is going to happen?"

"Nobody can leave this house for a few days," Parker told her, "that's the problem. If we could all just split now, go our separate ways, they'd lock us up here and take off, and that would be it. But you know this island's shut down, they're checking every car on every bridge, every boat in the water, they'll keep it up for three or four days."

"I know," she said.

"I'm going to make Melander itchy after a while," Parker said. "Just by being here."

"And you can't leave, not now," she said. "Or could you? Could we leave together? We wouldn't tell anybody."

He was already shaking his head. "They don't want us loose. They want us under control. And for now, that means here. Later on, it could mean dead."

"But not this morning, you think."

"Parker!" Ross's voice called up the stairwell. "You two up?"

"Yes," Parker called. Leslie stooped to pull her shoe back on.

"Come on downstairs."

Low, Parker said, "Now we'll find out."

5

Ross led them to the dining room, where Melander sat at the table with his back to the sea. The guns were gone from the table, and in their place were a box of doughnuts, a coffeepot, pound box of sugar, quart of half-and-half, white china cups, metal spoons, paper plates, and paper napkins. The shotguns leaned against the wall in a corner. The automatics were out of sight, probably being worn by the three. On a side table were three black mesh pouches attached to belts; Parker caught a glint of gold through the mesh. Carlson wasn't in sight.

Ross had gone into the room first, followed by Leslie, then Parker, so he was too late to stop it when Melander gestured to the chair on his left and said, "Have a seat, Claire. You don't mind if we're informal here, do you?"

247

She was moving with small steps, arms against her sides; holding it in. "No, that's all right," she said, and went over to sit where Parker had salted the Sentinel.

"Take a seat," Ross told Parker, while Melander said to Leslie, "I'm glad. We can all be pals. I'm Boyd, and that's Jerry. Hal's in the kitchen, trying to figure out the stove. Maybe you could help him later."

Parker, sitting to Melander's right, opposite Leslie, said, "Claire's not too much for stoves."

"No?" Melander grinned and shrugged. "Okay, fine. Either Hal figures it out, or he blows us all up." He gestured at the things on the table. "This is it for breakfast. Help yourselves."

Leslie looked uncertainly at Parker, who pushed the doughnut box toward her, saying, "Go ahead."

The coffeepot was near Parker. Melander said, "Parker, why don't you pour for her?"

"Claire likes to do that for herself," he said, and pushed the coffeepot toward her, too, because they might think it strange that he didn't know if his Claire took milk or sugar in her coffee.

She took it black, as did Parker, and they both took doughnuts, as Melander continued the conversation, saying, "Now, Parker, what are we gonna do about you?"

"Hold me until you leave," Parker said, and sensed movement behind him. That would be Carlson, coming in from the kitchen. Parker faced Melander but kept aware of Leslie; her reaction would let him know if Carlson had anything in mind. He said, "Then you'll get your money from the fences, and you'll send me what you owe me, and that's the end of it."

Behind him, Carlson said, "Forgive and forget, is that it?"

"No," Parker said, still talking to Melander. "I don't forgive, and I don't forget, but I don't waste time on the past, either. I won't work with you people again, but if you pay me my money I won't think about you anymore, either."

"That would be nice," Melander said. "We were talking about that last night, Hal and Jerry and me, how we didn't like the idea of you thinking about us."

"Showing up here," Carlson said. He was still behind Parker, not coming into view.

Parker kept looking at Melander. "This is where my money is," he said.

Melander laughed. He was buying Parker's story, though maybe Carlson wasn't. He said, "This is where your money is."

"That's right."

"What happens if we would have screwed up on the job? If we went up there and something went wrong?"

"I'd try to come in, get what I can."

Carlson, back there, said, "And help us out?"

"Not a chance," Parker said.

"I just wish," Melander said, "you were a more easy-going guy," and door chimes sounded.

Everybody in the room tensed. Carlson stepped

forward to Parker's right, looking at him, saying, "You got friends?"

"Only you people."

Melander said, "Jerry, take a look."

Ross hurried from the room while Carlson crossed to pick up two of the shotguns, bringing one to Melander, neither shotgun pointed exactly at anybody.

Stupid with fear, mouth open, Leslie stared at Parker, and Ross ducked back into the room: "It's cops!"

"For Christ's sake, why?" Carlson complained, glaring at Parker.

Parker said, "They're searching the island. Hello, Mr. Householder, you see anybody looked suspicious?"

Melander laughed and got to his feet, handing his shotgun back to Carlson as he said, "Everybody I see looks suspicious. I'm the householder." He left the room, smoothing his hair back.

Carlson and Ross went to stand to both sides of the parlor doorway, where they'd be able to hear. Parker waved a hand to get Leslie's attention, then pointed to her side of the table. She stared at him, not getting it. He tapped his temple: *Think.* Carlson and Ross wouldn't be distracted forever.

"Hello, Officers, what can I do for you?"

"Mr. George Roderick?"

"Yes, sir, that's me."

Parker put both hands under the table, gesturing that his hands were touching the underside, then again pointed at her side of the table.

"May we come in?"

"Sure. Could I ask—"

"Are you moving in or out, sir?"

At last she reached under her table, and her eyes widened.

"Moving in. Slowly, slowly."

"I suppose that would explain it."

Parker patted the air with palms down: *Don't move it yet.*

"Explain what?"

"You are aware of the robbery last night."

"Robbery? No, what robbery?"

"Mr. Roderick, a massive jewel theft and fire took place last night just up the road from here, and you don't *know* about it?"

"No, I'm sorry, I don't have a TV here, I don't even have a radio. I stayed home and read last night. I didn't—"

"You don't have a phone, either."

"No, I don't—it isn't in yet."

"We're phoning residents, asking if anyone saw anything, but you don't have a phone."

"No, not yet."

"You haven't applied for a phone."

"No, I haven't got a—"

"There's a Dumpster out here, but you have no contractor. No one's doing work on the property."

"Officer, I live mostly in Texas. There've been business problems there recently. I've been delayed in—"

"How many of you are staying here, Mr. Roderick?"

"At the moment, just me. My family's still—"

A different cop voice said, "Someone else came into the living room, went back out again. I saw it through the window."

"That was me," Melander said, still sounding affable, while Carlson and Ross were getting more and more edgy, hands flexing on the shotguns. "I had my coffee cup in my hand, went back to—"

"It wasn't you," the second cop voice said. "It was somebody shorter."

The first cop, sounding tougher, less polite, said, "Mr. Roderick, how many of you are in the house right now?"

"Just me, I'm telling—"

"Mr. Roderick, I'm afraid I'm going to have to search the house."

"I don't see why. I'm just a guy from Texas trying to fix up this—"

"And we'll have to begin with a search of your person, sir."

"Me? Search *me*?"

"Sir, if you'll lean against the wall, arms spread . . ."

It was now. Parker snapped his fingers to get Leslie's attention, and gestured she should toss him the gun. Carlson heard the snap, saw the gesture, saw the Sentinel come up from under the table in Leslie's two hands, a piece of clear tape still curling away from it, and he swung the shotgun around to shoot at Leslie, trigger going *click* as he squeezed.

Leslie flinched and *screamed* and fired the Sentinel, the flat *crack* of it bouncing in the room, the bullet missing Carlson, beelining somewhere into the living room, where the cops and Melander were.

Parker was on his feet, turning in a quick circle to his left, away from the doorway, reaching for the chairback behind him with his left hand. The pains in his torso drove knives into him, shot arcs of lightning across his vision, popped the sweat beads onto his forehead, but he kept turning, picking up the chair at the end of his left arm, swinging it in a loop that intersected with Ross, who had already fired his shotgun uselessly twice at Parker's head. The chair knocked him off balance to his right, into the doorway.

There was already shooting out there. Melander had probably drawn his automatic when he saw the situation going to hell, and had gone down pulling a trigger that just wouldn't deliver.

Ross reeled into the doorway space to the living room, clutching the shotgun, and was brought up short by a sudden squadron of bullets that knocked him backward, knocked the shotgun from his hands, knocked him to the ground.

Leslie had emptied the Sentinel, two-handed, into Carlson, who sprawled in a seated position on the floor against the wall, gaping at her, stupefied.

Parker clapped once, to get her attention. When she stared at him, glassy-eyed, he pointed to himself, fast, urgent, then violently shook his head. *I'm not here, I don't exist, I'm not part of it.* She managed an openmouthed nod, and he turned, grabbed the three pouches full of jewelry, and ran.

253

But he couldn't run. His body wasn't up to it; he was reeling from what he'd already done. He was one room ahead of them and couldn't go much farther.

He made it to the terrace. The morning sun glared dead ahead, breathing its humidity on him, sapping the rest of his strength.

They weren't pursuing anybody; they didn't know there was anybody else to pursue. They were staying with the mess they already had. But he couldn't just wander the beach, physically battered, carrying the loot from the robbery.

To the left was the chain-link fence he'd climbed the first time he'd come here, with the neighbor's sea grape crowding against it on the inside. Parker went to the corner of the terrace, looped the three pouch belts through his own belt, and went down the neighbor's side of the fence.

It was slow going, for many reasons. He didn't want to break a lot of branches, leave a trail straight to himself. He was bulky and cumbersome and the jewelry pouches kept snagging on branches and leaves. And his body kept trying to pass out.

At the bottom, the tangled stringy trunks were a failed Boy Scout knot. Years of dead leaves had made a mush of the ground. The air was cooler, but just as wet. A foot from the fence, you couldn't see the fence or the ocean beyond it.

Parker, feeling darkness iris in around his eyes, sank slowly into crotches and curves of branch until he'd given over his entire weight to the tree, as though he'd been hanging there forever and it had grown around him. He'd done what he could do. Arms around a trunk, cheek against a branch, he let the iris close.

6

Darkness and cramping, forcing him to be conscious. He tried to move, to ease the cramps, but he was all tangled in branches and leaves. Too dark to see where he was or what he could do.

He stopped the useless moving about. He ignored the cramps, in his ribs, in his legs, and took a slow deep breath while he oriented himself. Where he was. What had happened.

He'd slept the day away, laced into a sea grape. They hadn't found him, so they hadn't looked for him or they *would* have found him, so Leslie's story—whatever it had been—had not included him.

Could he get up out of here? The first thing was to try to stand, untie himself from this tree. Reaching this way and that for handholds, his knuckles brushed the chain-link fence, and he grabbed onto it, used it to pull himself forward and then upward until he was vertical and could try to do something about the cramps.

For the torso, just slow breathing, slow and regular breathing, holding it in. For the legs, flexing them and flexing them and flexing them, waiting it out. Until finally only the familiar pains in his chest were left, a little worse than before, but not crippling.

He could see nothing, but he could feel the three jewelry pouches, still looped onto his belt in front and on the left side. He still had hold of the fence, and now he began to climb it, slowly, with long pauses. The legs threatened to bind up on him again, and the breathing was very thick and soupy, but he kept moving upward, a bit at a time, and finally came out onto the terrace behind the late Mr. Roderick's house. He sprawled there, on his back.

Light. A quarter-moon and many stars. The hushing sound of the ocean, rising and falling. No other sound and no other light.

Finally, when he felt he had the strength for it, he gathered his arms and legs under himself, and levered himself upward, and used the protective wrought-iron fence for support, and then he was on his feet.

The house was dark, its many glass doors dully reflecting the bright night sky. Something ribbonlike fluttered over there, horizontal, at waist height, and when he moved slowly closer to the building it was a yellow police crime-scene tape. They'd sealed the house.

How sealed was it? He needed this house. In slow

stages, with many pauses, he worked his way around to the front, where the Dumpster still loomed in the moonlight and more crime-scene tape semaphored in the night breeze. But there were no vehicles, no guards. The crime at the crime scene, as far as the law was concerned, was over.

It took longer this time to find the suction-cup handles, but eventually he did, and got into the house the same way as before, but feeling the damage to his body even worse. He did pass out, for a while, lying on the floor inside the house, the window open beside him, but then he came out of it and stood and finished the job, tossing the suction-cup handles outside again, hoping to never need those anymore. He reinserted the loose pane of glass, and then he was inside.

The alarm pad by the front door gleamed its red warning, but had the police checked to be certain the alarm hadn't been tampered with? No, they hadn't. If the alarm was doing its job, his opening the window would have set it off.

And if he were his usual self, he'd have been much more cautious about coming in here. He could see that the physical toll was beginning to make him careless, sloppy in his thinking. He couldn't let that happen.

It wasn't really possible to search the place in this darkness, even if he had the strength. But the air had the flat silence of an empty house, and he was sure he was alone.

The same furniture was still in the dining room,

though disarranged; nobody had bothered to pick up the chair Parker had knocked over. In the kitchen, the refrigerator was still full of food. There was cold fried chicken in there, and there was beer. He ate and drank, and then curled up on the floor and slept.

1

On Monday they came to clean out the house, where he'd been trying to recuperate since Saturday night. They didn't expect to find anybody inside the place, so Parker had no trouble keeping out of their way. They were two plainclothes detectives, one bored uniform, and a crew of movers. The detectives would check each room, okay it, and the movers would label everything and take it all out.

Having expected something like this, Parker had already made a stash of provisions, hidden in the unfinished part of the attic. In there were a razor and shaving cream and comb and some clothing, all things the dead heisters had left behind, plus an unopened box of cereal, a plastic bag of rolls, two cans of tuna, and half a dozen bottles of beer. But if they were going to shut this house down completely he wouldn't be able to stay much longer.

After they left, he came down to see what they'd taken, which was all the furniture, all the personal possessions, all the leftover food. The refrigerator was there, but had been switched off and the door propped open. There was still water and still electricity, so he started the refrigerator and put the beer and rolls in it.

What he was waiting for was Leslie. She'd come back, he knew she would. She'd figure some way to get back to this house, if only out of curiosity. Or, more likely, to try to find his trail. One way or another, she would show up here, and that's what he had to count on, because he needed her assistance just one more time. He knew he couldn't just walk out of here and down the road, looking the way he did. He wouldn't get half a mile before some cop would stop to ask questions. Any question at all.

Wednesday afternoon. He was spending most of his waking time seated on the floor on the second-floor terrace, out of sight of anybody on the beach, but in the open air, giving his body a chance to relax, to heal itself. He had all the interior doors open in the house, and the door to the terrace open, so he'd hear if anybody came in.

Midafternoon, the terrace now in the building's shadow. He felt hungry, but otherwise not bad. The breathing was better, the ribs less painful. The bandages were now almost a week old, but he didn't want to remove them or fuss with them because he didn't have any replacements.

261

He heard the front door shut, and rose, grunting a little. In the doorway, he could look straight down the staircase to the front hall, where he saw Leslie just disappearing to the right. Going to switch off the useless alarm.

He stepped through the doorway, leaned on the railing at the head of the stairs, waited. She came into view again down there, looking around, as though deciding what to do first. Softly, he called, "You alone?"

She lifted her startled face, saw him up there. "My God! I thought you were a thousand miles from here!"

"Not yet. Wait there, I'll come down."

He went down, and they sat together on the staircase, and he noted the clump of keys in her hand. "It's okay you being here?"

She grinned, pleased with herself. "I've got the exclusive," she said.

"I don't follow."

"The house reverted to its former owner," she explained, "so it's on the market again. I'm a heroine, so I've got the exclusive listing." She grinned at him, as though bringing him a present. "No one is going to come into this house unless they're with me."

"That's good," he said. "But I can't stay here. Are they still doing traffic stops?"

"No," she said. "They think the fourth man escaped with the jewelry somewhere else."

"Fourth man?"

"They searched the house all day Saturday and

didn't find the jewelry, so there must be a fourth man."

"All right."

"They think the three who came here gave this fourth man the jewelry somewhere along the way, and I'm pretty sure they *think* he's somebody locally prominent, but nobody's saying so."

Parker stretched his lips in a grin. "Now it's an inside job," he said.

"Exactly," she said, grinning back, but then her expression clouded, and she said, "Except for that sheriff. Farley."

"He's still around?"

"He's decided," she told him, "that the fourth man was Daniel Parmitt, and the other three got him out of the hospital because they needed him in their plan. Nobody else cares about Daniel Parmitt or thinks he had anything to do with the robbery, only Farley. He thinks Parmitt had a boat or something. He keeps trying to find somebody to tell that story to, but the police here think he's just a small-town jerk from the Everglades."

"He's a small-town jerk, but he's sharp," Parker said. "What story did *you* tell?"

"I said I thought this house had been abandoned, because there was never anybody around, and I wanted the opportunity to sell it if it was on the market, and I even thought *you* might be a prospect."

"Parmitt."

"Right. And I came here, and it was unlocked, and there was nobody home. And I was still looking

263

around when these three terrifying men in wet suits came in and kidnapped me. And I didn't see them carrying any jewels, then or ever."

"Good."

"They held me overnight, and then they gave me breakfast in the morning, and I found that little gun taped under the table, I have no idea where it came from. There was still tape on the gun when I gave it to the police, and they found the rest under the table."

"Good."

"I told them I was afraid to touch it at first, but then the police arrived, and I thought they were going to go away again and not rescue me, so that's why I pulled the gun out to shoot it to attract their attention."

"That's good," Parker said. "And you're a local, solid reputation, the story's good enough, so it might be true."

"They believe me," she insisted.

He shrugged. "Why not? What do they think about the guns being rigged?"

She looked confused. "Rigged?"

"Their guns didn't shoot," Parker pointed out.

"That's right," she said in wonder, "I forgot about that. I thought I was *dead* when that man pointed that rifle at me, but then it didn't shoot."

"None of them did," Parker said. "What do the police say?"

"Nothing. There hasn't been a word about that."

Parker thought it over. "Did nobody notice? Everything going by so fast. Or somebody noticed, and they decided, why should we tell everybody we killed three guys that couldn't shoot back? Okay, just so they're not making a big deal out of it."

"They're not."

He said, "You know that bank account of mine in San Antonio."

She shook her head. "I tried," she said, "on Monday."

"Oh, yeah?"

"I went through a lot of trouble," she told him. "I wanted some money."

"Sure."

"The man was very nice," she said, "but he told me there was a temporary hold on that account, and he couldn't ship me any more money."

So Parmitt was gone for good. "All right. You've got some of the ten grand left."

"Some," she admitted.

"You've still got my clothing sizes. I need some Daniel Parmitt clothes, clothes I don't look like an ex-con in."

"I bet you are an ex-con," she said.

"Polo shirt. Khakis. Tassel loafers. Sunglasses. White yachting cap."

"I love your disguises," she said.

"Wait here," he told her, and stood, and went into the kitchen, where the circuit breaker box stood on the wall beside the window over the sink. He opened the metal cover and snaked out the painted wooden one-by-four running underneath it that

265

he'd loosened the other day. Under there, inside the wall, the three jewelry pouches hung from the Romex wire cables leading out of the box. He removed them, put everything back, and carried them to the front hall, where Leslie abruptly got to her feet at the sight of them, as though she'd seen the Queen walk by.

"Is that *it*?"

"All of it. Will it fit in your bag?"

Like most career women, Leslie's brown leather bag was outsize, more utilitarian than fashionable. She said, "Let me just get a couple of these maps and things out of here. You're *giving* it all to me?"

"You're holding it," he told her. "You take it home, you hide it someplace where your mother and your sister won't find it, and someday soon, a few weeks or a month from now, a guy's gonna come around and say he's from Daniel Parmitt. Only first I'll phone you, and I'll tell you what name he's using and what he looks like."

She was very solemn, nodding at each thing he said. "All right."

"He'll take the stuff away," Parker said. "He and I'll work out a price. Then he'll come back and give you one-third. Okay?"

"One-third." She was still awed. "How much would that be?"

"We're guessing four hundred thousand for you, might be less."

"Not much less."

"No."

She hefted the bag, her maps and Filofax in her other hand. "You're trusting me with this?"

"It isn't trust, Leslie," he said. "What are you gonna do with it? Go to a pawnshop?"

"I think there's a reward."

"Not four hundred thousand. And then you'd have to explain where you got it. No, you'll hold on to it, and you'll take the four."

"I certainly will," she said. The awe was being replaced by a broad grin. "This sure worked out, didn't it?"

"For some of us. Can you come back tonight around eight? With my new clothes."

"Sure."

"And drive me down to Miami."

"Okay. Is that where Claire is?"

He said, "You don't want to know about Claire, Leslie."

"Of course I do," she said.

He looked at her, and decided to finish that part once and for all. "Claire is the only house I ever want to be in," he said. "All her doors and windows are open, but only for me."

A blush climbed Leslie's cheeks, and she stepped back, looking confused, as though a door had just slammed in her face. "You're probably anxious to see her again," she said, mumbling, going through the motions. "I'll see you at eight."

8

Except, no. Not ten minutes after Leslie left, with Parker once more seated on the upstairs terrace floor, back against the wall of the house, he heard the sound of the front door, and when he stood up to look, it was Farley. The Snake River sheriff, in uniform, right hand on his holstered firearm, creeping cautiously into the house, looking every which way at once.

Followed Leslie. Thought she'd lead him to Parmitt, or to somebody else connected with the jewelry robbery. But giving Parker an opportunity to deal with some of the problems he still had.

It wasn't possible to go through the house, Farley was too alert for that. Parker went down the corner of the wall from the terrace, the way he'd come up from the lower terrace the first time he'd entered this house, and moved as fast as he could around to the front, where he saw Farley's official sheriff's car parked by the front door.

It wasn't locked, and the driver's window was open so it wouldn't get too hot and stuffy while Farley was away. Parker got into the passenger seat in front, read the owner's manual for a while, and twenty minutes later Farley came out of the house, grimacing in frustration. When he saw Parker seated in his car he at first looked enraged, then triumphant, as though he'd been proved right about something.

He came around and got behind the wheel and said, "You were in there."

"In where? In that house? No, I've been out here. I followed you. I wanted to talk to you."

Farley's glare meant no-nonsense-pal. He said, "You were in there, and the Mackenzie woman came to see you there."

"Who? Oh, Leslie. No, I haven't seen Leslie since she came to visit me at the hospital." Parker made a crooked-face grin and said, "I think I scared her that time."

"She helped you *escape* from the hospital."

"What, that *woman*? Don't be stupid."

Farley didn't like being called stupid, but he knew he wasn't on secure ground here, so he said, "Have it your own way," and turned to start the engine.

Mild, Parker said, "Where we going?"

"Snake River, of course," Farley said as he thumbed his window shut. "I'm arresting you."

"For what?"

"For running away from the hospital."

269

"That's no crime," Parker told him. "Ask the hospital if there's any charges they want to press against me."

The engine was running, the air conditioner blowing its cold breeze into the car, but Farley hadn't put it in gear. He glowered at Parker, thinking it over, and then said, "You're mixed up in that big jewel robbery."

"Wrong again."

"Don't tell me. I *know*."

"In the first place," Parker said, "that isn't your case, and in the second place, nobody who *is* working on that case thinks I had anything to do with it, and you know it."

"They're wrong," Farley said.

"Everybody's wrong but you."

"It happens," Farley said.

Parker nodded, looking at him. "Happen often?"

"Oh, fuck you, Parmitt," Farley snapped, and pointed an angry finger at him. "And that's another thing. You aren't any Daniel Parmitt."

"Everybody knows that," Parker said. As Farley gaped at him, he gestured at the house. "Why don't we go sit in there and get comfortable? There's nobody home, is there?"

"It's empty, it's got no furniture in it, as you damn well know."

"Oh, really?" Parker looked at the house, shrugged and said, "Then we might as well stay here. For a cop, you're goddam incurious."

"About what?" Farley demanded. He was ready at this point to take offense at just about anything.

"At why I'm sitting in your car," Parker told him.

That took Farley aback. He thought about it and said, "You didn't want me following you."

"You weren't following me, I was following you."

"Oh, goddammit, Parmitt, John Doe, whoever the hell you are, all *right*. Why are you in my car, if not to get arrested for a dozen different things I can think of?"

"Don't embarrass yourself, Farley," Parker advised him. "If you had any case at all, I'd be in cuffs right now."

Farley sat back against his door to look Parker up and down. "You've been getting me riled up on purpose," he decided.

"You started it on your own."

"I did. So you did it like a firebreak, I guess, to calm me down. Okay, I'm calm. Why are you in my car?"

"Because I want to know how you're doing with the guy who's hiring people to kill me."

Farley nodded. "All right," he said. "It's a good reason."

"I know it is. How are you doing?"

"Well, the Chicago police—" At Parker's look, he made a sour face and said, "Yeah, Chicago's taken over now. Bernson, the guy we caught in the hospital—"

"That his name? I only heard you got somebody."

"Edward Bernson. A professional killer, according

271

to the Chicago people. One of the guns on him tied him to two other murders over the last couple years. When we saw we had him cold, he flipped."

"And gave you the name of the guy that hired him."

"No, the go-between. It's a lawyer in Chicago named Gilma Yard, and now the Chicago police are looking into it. They think she's like a clearinghouse or an agency for killers, for hit men. They're not even sure that's her name, but her files are full of stuff that's gonna clear up a lot of murders around the country."

Parker said, "This Gilma Yard, she isn't the principal? She's just the one that runs the string of killers?"

"That's how it looks."

"And they haven't flipped her."

"Not yet. She's stonewalling, and she's a lawyer, and she seems to think she can skate out of it. I don't know if she can, but right now they've got her in protective custody in case there's any customers out there that wouldn't like to be mentioned."

"So it's still that nobody knows who's hiring these people that are trying to gun me down."

"Well, *you* must know," Farley told him.

"I don't."

Farley shook his head. "That isn't possible. You must have *some* idea why you—"

"No. We'll get to that," Parker promised, "but what's happening with this lawyer and her files? Don't they at least have somebody who *could* be the guy?"

272

Reluctantly, Farley said, "Yes."

"In Chicago?"

"No, in Tulsa, Oklahoma."

"We do get around," Parker said. "Who is this guy?"

Farley gave him an exasperated look. "Just given the wild chance that you *don't* know who's gunning for you," he said, "why should I give you a name? So you can go out to Oklahoma and deal with him yourself? Level with me and let the law deal with him."

"I want the law to deal with him."

"Well, the law can't," Farley said, "not so far, because there's no connection between the man in Tulsa and Daniel Parmitt. But why should there be, when you *aren't* Daniel Parmitt and we don't know who you are? If we knew who you really were, we'd know the link."

"Sheriff Farley," Parker said, "I'm going to make you an offer."

Farley thought about that. He squinted at his white car hood, baking in the sun. He adjusted the air conditioner down a notch. He said, "I can at least listen to it."

"I will tell you the link between this man and me," Parker said. "It's a stupid link, but it's the only one there is. You will tell me the name of the guy in Tulsa, and then I'll give every law enforcement agency in the country a year to bring him down. You won't need a month, I think, given the guy. But if you all fuck up, in a year and a day I kill him."

Farley said, "Why do you want to do it that way?"

"Because he's already been too much of a distrac-

273

tion. Because I don't want to have to think about him anymore."

"The man had you *shot*. You don't feel any desire to go deal with him yourself?"

"Why? You people are better equipped than me to be sure he's the right guy. And I want him *out* of my life, not *in* my life. And the other thing, Sheriff, just between you and me, I don't want you on my back-trail anymore, either. You go live your life in Snake River, and I'll go live my life somewhere else."

"If I see you again—"

"You won't."

Farley thought it over. He said, "If I took you in, took your prints, asked you questions a few days, showed you to my friends at the FBI, I bet we'd come up with a lot of answers we'd like."

"Sheriff," Parker said, "if you make a single move in that direction, the two of us in the car here together, you're a much more stupid man than I think you are."

Farley considered that. "I'm armed," he pointed out.

Parker held his hands up between them, fingers half-curled. "So am I."

"Jesus, you've got gall!"

Parker lowered his hands. "Do we have a deal?"

"You'll tell me the link between you and the man in Tulsa, and you'll keep away from him for a year, and we should have enough to get the goods on him."

"And," Parker said, "you'll tell me his name."

"Zulf Masters," Farley said.

"Zulf Masters."

"All anybody knows is, he's rich, everybody thinks from oil. He's in real estate, office buildings and shopping centers, all through Oklahoma and Kansas and Missouri."

"That's laundered money," Parker said. "It didn't come from oil. Zulf Masters," he repeated, in case he'd have to remember it later.

"Nobody's sure if that's *his* real name, either," Farley said.

"It isn't," Parker said.

"These are very dubious people, Parmitt," Farley said. "Bad as you."

"Take notes, Sheriff."

Farley had pen and notepad as part of the console between the front seats. He obediently picked them up and said, "Go ahead."

"In Galveston, Texas," Parker told him, "there was a man named Julius Norte."

"Was."

Parker spelled the name. "Sometime in the last month he was murdered. I think by the same two that shot me."

"Oh ho," Farley said.

"Norte created ID for people."

"Like Daniel Parmitt."

"That's right. He did very good stuff, you could do background checks, whatever. Only the credit history wouldn't be there."

"You traveled with your birth certificate," Farley

said. "That snagged at me, but I didn't think it through."

Parker said, "If the Chicago cops are right about this guy in Tulsa, he got his name from Norte. And whoever he really is, some South American warlord or drug dealer or whoever, he doesn't want anybody who can link the new guy to the old guy. So he must have had plastic surgery, and he probably killed the surgeon. He killed Norte. And because I was there, I happened to be there at the time, he's trying to kill me. It was whoever was gonna be Norte's customer that day was gonna have this guy breathing down his back."

Farley looked up from his notepad. "That's it? That's all of it? You were with Norte at the wrong minute, and this fellow wants you dead?"

"I think he's somebody comes from a former life where making people dead was the solution to most problems."

Farley said, "If we can prove the Zulf Masters identity is a fake, we can get through to the real guy."

"The one thing Norte couldn't do," Parker told him, "was the Social Security number. He said he didn't have the access to the legit files."

"That'll bring him down," Farley said. "You're right, we won't need a year."

"He's going to be some stinking piece of work when you find out who he really is."

Farley laughed. "Worse than you and me?"

"Worse than you," Parker said. "You going back to Snake River now?"

"Naturally. So I can call Chicago."

"Drop me off in Miami Beach."

"That's out of my way."

"Not that far. And you can give me a quarter for a phone call."

Farley shook his head. "You don't lack for nerve, Parmitt, I'll give you that."

Forty minutes south of Palm Beach on Interstate 95, Farley said, "It isn't Mackenzie."

Parker looked at him. "What isn't Mackenzie?"

"Who you're meeting in Miami Beach."

"Farley," Parker said, "you've got that woman on your mind. You've got the itch for her, haven't you?"

"Don't be stupid," Farley said, glaring at the traffic on 95. "I'm a happily married man."

"They all are," Parker said, and Farley didn't talk about Leslie anymore.

Driving down Collins Avenue in Miami Beach, Farley said, "Where do you want to get off?"

"Anywhere at all," Parker said.

"No, I know you're still hurting, you don't want to walk a lot, I'll let you off wherever you say."

"Anywhere along Collins is fine by me," Parker said.

Farley laughed. "You don't want to give me one clue."

Parker looked at the hard-bodied girls on roller skates, weaving in and out among the retirees. Everything that was extreme was here.

277

Farley found a fire hydrant and stopped next to it. "I give up," he said. "Hold on, here's your quarter." It came from a cup on the dashboard.

"Thanks."

"You know, Parmitt," Farley said as Parker opened the door, "it's kind of an anticlimax for me, you just walking off like this."

"Yeah?"

"I'll always wonder," Farley said, "if I could have taken you."

"Look on the bright side," Parker told him. "This way, you have an always."